For the Love of You

Candace Shaw

Edited by Melissa M. Ringsted
Cover Art: Yocla Designs

Shaw Press
Atlanta, Georgia

ISBN-13: 978-1530442850
ISBN-10: 1530442850

PROLOGUE

Dr. Garrett Braxton leaned against the column and sipped his champagne while he gazed intently at the long-legged, mocha beauty that at the moment was the only thing in his vision. Sure there were people in front of him on the dance floor, including the blushing bride and groom who were everyone else's focus. However, the wedding coordinator was the only woman who held his attention as she strutted around the Memphis Cultural Arts Center's banquet hall, making sure everything ran smoothly for Justin and Shelbi Richardson's wedding reception. While Zaria Richardson had a knack for remaining calm and reserved, whenever Garrett locked her stare with his and raised a slick grin, she'd either roll her eyes or turn her head in a way that her sheets and sheets of black tresses, which fell to her waist, would cover the side of her face. A strain pressed against Garrett's pants at the mere thought of grasping all of her mane while trailing his tongue along her graceful neck and back to her tempting, kissable lips.

Sipping his drink, he nodded his head in her direction—it caused her to purse her lips and saunter away in her four-inch heels, adding even more height to her already five-foot-seven frame. Garrett chuckled and moved along the crowd, smiling and acknowledging people he knew until he reached his best friend since medical school, Dr. Sean Arrington, who was busy typing on his cell phone.

"What's with the serious expression? Something wrong with one of your clients?"

Sean glanced up with an amused smirk, then back to the screen. "Got these two honeys texting me. Both want to come over later on, so I'm trying to convince them we can all have fun. You wanna hang?"

"Naw. I'm good."

Sean twisted his lips to the side. "Uh huh. I see you scoping out Ms. Diva."

Garrett shrugged and downed the rest of his Moet. "I just like teasing with her. Zaria is hella sexy when she's mad." Wanting to change the subject, he glanced around the room and spotted another topic to discuss. "Can you believe Rasheed Vincent caught the garter?" he asked, referring to the groom's best friend.

"Better him than me. I have no intention of marrying anytime soon. However, if he keeps eyeing my sister all night like she's a piece of meat, he's gonna have to answer to me," Sean stated seriously.

"Man, he and Bria are just friends. You know he's a player for life like you."

Dipping his gaze at his beeping cell phone, a wicked grin emerged across Sean's face. "Yep, and the two honeys have agreed to my request. Sure you don't want to come?"

Garrett barely heard what his friend asked when he caught Zaria's dark, tempting eyes flash his way as she ushered the bride and her two sisters out of the reception hall. "Nope, I already have plans."

Zaria's heels had barely touched the hardwood in his foyer before Garrett meshed her body with his, and slammed his mouth on her juicy lips in a wild, aggressive kiss. He shut the door by backing her against it, and travelled his hands roughly down her side until they clutched her shapely hips. Letting out a fervent gasp, she wrapped her leg around his torso, and he raised the hem of her fitted, black dress around her stomach to expose black satin panties.

"You're late," he muttered against her neck while sucking on it hard.

Pushing him away, she eased her dress and panties down to the floor and stepped out of them while leaving on her heels. "Stop trying to brand me." She pulled him back by the collar and gritted her teeth. "I don't belong to you."

Chuckling, he unbuckled his belt and pants. Reaching into his pocket, he slid out a packet and opened it as a sexy smize crossed her lips, which were swollen from his kiss.

"And yet your body responds to me as if you do." Lifting her leg again, he teased his rod around her opening before plunging in with one fluid stroke. She grasped his shoulders tightly as amorous moans continued to escape her lips while he thrust into her over and over.

Garrett loved hearing Zaria for there was no faking from her. If she enjoyed it she always let him know with her mouth, hands, and the beautifully erotic faces she'd make. If she didn't, she'd demand what she wanted, how she wanted it, and he always obliged. She wasn't a woman afraid of her sexual side. With her he never had to hold back.

Zaria strolled out of the bathroom wearing his tuxedo shirt opened with the bow tie hanging loose around the collar. Her perky breasts bounced as she moved toward the bed and Garrett couldn't wait to get a hold of her chocolate mounds once more. Focusing his gaze to her belly button and continuing below to the neatly trimmed triangle, he licked his tongue across his bottom lip as his mind wandered to what he wanted to do next to her. She raised a cocky eyebrow at his gesture as if she'd read his mind, and crawled seductively up his naked body until she sat on his chest. He loved being intimate with her because her wild sex drive matched his. They both relished being in control of their secret rendezvous sessions, and he highly enjoyed when she would take over the reins.

Reaching up, he unclamped the clip that held her hair in a tousled, sexy mess on the top of her head. It fell sensually around her face and cascaded down to her elbows. He intertwined his fingers into her thick tresses. "You know I prefer it down."

Zaria scrunched her nose and bent her head over him, resting her forehead on his. "You don't run me, Doc," she reminded, pointing her finger on his bare chest.

Chuckling, he slapped her bottom. He always enjoyed her sassy mouth … especially when it was on his. "Oh no? I think I just finished *running* your freaky self up and down the front door."

She swished her lips to the side before letting out a yawn and rolling off of him. Lying next to him, she settled in his embrace. "It's been a long day. No, a long week with all of the wedding activities, and its Christmas Eve. I've had to squeeze in shopping, along with helping my parents set up the tree and decorations."

Glancing at the clock on the nightstand, he kissed her forehead. It was just a few minutes past midnight. "Actually, it's Christmas Day. Merry Christmas."

"Oh." Shrugging, she paused and sat up on her elbow to stare down at him. "Merry Christmas. So why didn't you bring your girlfriend to the wedding?"

Taken aback by the question, he wrinkled his brow. They rarely discussed their dating lives unless it was necessary. "Um … maybe because I don't have a girlfriend."

"But you're dating someone, right?" She sat all the way up and tucked her legs underneath her. "What's her name? Shelia?"

Zaria fastened a few of the buttons of his shirt much to his chagrin. He was ready to slip it off of her and slide back into her, not talk about his barely there dating life. Since he'd met her a few months ago while planning a scholarship fundraiser event for the Distinguished Men of Memphis, they'd established a sex only relationship after a heated discussion in her office about centerpieces that resulted in sex on her desk.

"I've been on a few dates with her, but we aren't exclusive and which you know. And I definitely wasn't going to bring her to a wedding. Women read too much into things like that."

"Humph, not me. I couldn't care less."

"I know." Drawing her to him, he kissed her softly. "You're a different kind of woman, Zaria."

"So have you slept with her yet, old man?"

He chuckled at her comment. She considered him old even though he was only thirty-two. "You wouldn't be here if I had."

"I know. Just making sure you're sticking to the agreement."

The agreement was to stop sleeping with each other if either one of them began to date someone exclusively. So far that hadn't happened. In a way he didn't want it to. He liked Zaria more than he cared to admit, and honestly wanted more than just a fling with her. But she'd been straight up in the beginning, stating that at age twenty-three she wanted to concentrate on her career and personal goals. She was the event planner for her cousin Justin's restaurant, but had aspirations of owning her own event planning company someday and that was her only focus.

Garrett released her from his embrace and reached over to the nightstand. Pulling a small, black velvet box out of the drawer, he handed it to her. "I have a gift for you."

She frowned as he handed her the box. "Oh ... I didn't know we were exchanging gifts." She slowly opened it and smiled as she pulled out a gold chain with a diamond Z on it. Her eyes sparkled and a genuine smile crossed her features.

"This is beautiful, but you didn't have to give me anything." Running her finger along the Z, she couldn't stop smiling as she unclasped the necklace and placed it around her neck.

"I know, but I remember you said you liked Carrie Bradshaw's 'Carrie' necklace on "Sex and the City" but that you would just want a Z. I saw it in the jewelry store while looking at watches for my dad, and I thought of you."

"Well, it's very sweet of you." She ran her fingers through her hair until it covered one side of her face. "Thank you, G." Closing the box, she reached over him to set it on the nightstand. Straddling his lap, she leaned over and kissed him gently on the lips. "And I have something for you."

He raised a wicked eyebrow at her sultry tone. "And what's that?"

"Another round with me."

He flipped her over—as she gasped and giggled at the same time—and landed his lips possessively over hers.

CHAPTER ONE

6 years later ...

"Do you really think that looks perfect?" Aggravated, Zaria slapped her hand on her forehead and ran her fingers through her hair as she glared at the man on the ladder who'd just draped a gardenia garland around one of the columns. Placing her hands on her hips, she swished her lips to the side. "It isn't hanging like the others, and it's throwing off my entire vision for this wedding that starts in a few hours."

"I'm sorry, Ms. Richardson."

"Don't be sorry, Chauncey. Just fix it. Precious Moments Events promises perfection, elegance, and class for every occasion. We don't half-ass anything."

Frustrated, she strutted across the wood planked floor while her inquisitive eyes perused the white-sheered tent one last time. Everything else was magnificently beautiful thanks to her fine eye for detail and creativity. Gardenia and rose garlands swooped the top of the tent, and two-feet tall centerpieces of white and fuchsia roses intertwined with ivy leaves cascaded from crystal vases.

"That's perfect, Chauncey," she called out.

Smiling, she sighed and exited the tent that faced the Atlantic Ocean of St. Simons Island, Georgia. It was indeed a perfect May day for a wedding. The sky was free of dark clouds, and even though there was a plan B in place for rain, there was none in the forecast.

"Zaria, there you are."

She turned to spot her baby cousin, and head event planner, Reagan Richardson strolling toward her. "Hey. How's the bride?" Zaria asked, nodding her head at the beach mansion where the bride's family resided.

"A nervous wreck, but her bridesmaids are calming her down. They're heading to the lighthouse in a few minutes to take pictures. Brooklyn is there now with the groom and the groomsmen, who will stay while the groom leaves with his father. I just hope they don't cross paths. If they take the routes I suggested they won't, but Brooklyn knows what to do."

"Of course. Everything is on schedule." She stopped when her cell phone vibrated on the clip attached to her jeans. Sliding it out, she groaned at the name and her heart skipped a few beats. *What's-his-face.* She hadn't spoken to *him* since she'd moved from Memphis a year ago to St. Simons to be a partner with Reagan's event planning company.

"What's wrong?" Reagan asked as the ladies trekked toward the tent.

"Oh, nothing." Zaria waved it off and let the call go to voicemail. She shifted the Z on her necklace back and forth to calm her nerves.

"Everything looks exquisite by the way. Your imagination never ceases to amaze me."

"Thanks, hon. I'm heading over to Jekyll Island to drop off the floral arrangements for the medical convention's opening reception tonight, and then I'm going home to crash. I've been here since four o' clock this morning. I'll see you bright and early tomorrow for the going away brunch. The centerpieces the bride's mother requested are safe in a spare bedroom. All I have to do is set them out before the guests arrive."

"Splendid. Maybe you'll meet a handsome doctor at the medical convention."

Zaria chuckled sarcastically. "I'll be sure to send him *your* way."

Once settled in the driver's seat of her Range Rover, Zaria frowned as her cell phone beeped indicating she had a voicemail. She was slightly curious as to why *he* was calling all of a sudden, but decided she could wait until she was at home with a glass of wine. Besides, he wasn't anyone important … or at least that's what she'd convinced herself of for the past year. They'd never dated—he was just a guy she hooked up with every blue moon for a few years in between a couple of boyfriends until she left Memphis. However, she'd thought of him during her late night quiet time because he was absolutely wonderful in bed and every other place that they'd had sex.

A strong force jolted through her at the thought of his hands and lips tantalizing her skin, especially his skilled tongue that always left her panting for more of it. He would ravish her as if he owned every single inch of her body, and in a way she'd almost believed it to be true. During the time she'd had a steady boyfriend for almost a year, she'd gone without seeing what's-his-face because of their agreement not to sleep together if they were in exclusive relationships. Zaria wasn't sure what he'd done to her, but whenever she would have sex with her boyfriend she was bored out of her mind. None of her hot spots came alive, and if she climaxed it was only because she would think about the last time she'd had sex with what's-his-face.

Biting her bottom lip, Zaria breathed in as she came to a stoplight. She shook her head at her amorous thoughts and glanced at her cell phone, which sat on the passenger seat, when it beeped again. Groaning, she grabbed it, shut it off, and tossed it into her tote bag. She had a job to do; not think about a man that she hated to admit had at one point become a weakness for her. Briefly, she'd even thought he'd make a good boyfriend considering he was attentive, romantic, and highly intelligent, all the traits she wanted in a man. However, he'd started to date someone exclusively and she decided she must've been insane for thinking they'd ever be more than occasional sex buddies.

Moments later she arrived at the Jekyll Island Convention Center and spotted her contact person as she entered the building, along with a man wheeling a cart her way. Even though Zaria didn't have anything to with the planning of the conference, she was commissioned to make four flower arrangements for the food tables at the opening reception.

There were plenty of men and women waiting in line to receive registration packets or standing around chatting. Reagan's joke of finding a doctor crossed her mind, and while there were some handsome ones eyeing her, she wasn't interested. Dating seemed to complicate her life, which was one of the reasons she steered away from it. She was only twenty-nine, and figured she would wait until her mid-thirties before settling down with one man, marrying, and having children—even though she couldn't picture herself being married. The thought irked her because she enjoyed her straightforward life. She made her own rules and adhered to them.

Zaria diverted her attention away from the doctors and smiled at Patricia Holder, one of the event planners for the conference center, as she approached.

"Hello, Zaria. Stunning as always, my love," Patricia complimented as the ladies hugged.

"Thank you. And you look fabulous, doll. The flowers are on ice in my SUV, and I received the final deposit in the account today so we're all set."

"Splendid. I ..."

Patricia's words became a jumbled blur when Zaria spotted a man gazing at her from the corner of her eye. Her heart sunk as she recognized the cool swagger of Dr. Garrett Braxton, or as he was listed in her cell phone what's-his-face. For a moment she didn't recognize him for she was used to his clean-shaven face and wavy hair. However, the short curly fro and the low-cut beard he sported was indeed sexy, and made his boyish look—which she always thought was cute—parlay him into a more mature appearance.

Now she knew why he'd called. He was in town for the medical convention which meant he wanted to see her, and from the rise of his devilish grin it also meant he wanted her. She tried to stay focused on Patricia's ramblings of how her week had been hell preparing for five hundred doctors and nurses, but Zaria's eyes diverted toward the ruggedly handsome man who was staring her down like she was a dessert he wanted to devour. And she wanted … no, needed him, too. It had been far too long, and since he was in town her thirsty drought could now be quenched. Her mouth watered at the thought, and she peeled her eyes away long enough to comprehend the conversation with her business associate.

Realizing Patricia had asked for the keys to her SUV, Zaria handed them to the man with the cart and told him where she'd parked. Patricia excused herself to check on a mishap and Zaria was finally able to exhale until Garrett strode her way wearing a delicious smile across his charismatic, sienna-shaded face. She hated that she was flustered for some reason. Men never unnerved her, but there was something about his demeanor that unraveled her all of a sudden.

"Hey, little lady. I see you heard my message and came rushing over to Jekyll," he teased. "You missed me, didn't you?"

Pursing her lips together, she frowned. "Wrong. I haven't listened to your voicemail. I'm here on business. Purely coincidental, and I didn't miss you. Haven't even thought you."

He drew her toward him. She suppressed a shudder as his six-foot-one frame engulfed her in his embrace and his familiar scent surrounded her. He wasn't an overly built man, but his lean, in-shape physique always made her feel protected and warm.

"Maybe it was fate."

Chuckling sarcastically, she gave him a haughty glare. "I don't think so, old man."

"Old man? You've never once complained about how this old man rocked your boat off and on for five years."

"Whatever. So how long are you going to be in town?" she asked, running over her schedule in her head for the next few days.

"Until Tuesday morning. I was hoping we could hang out ... unless you're seeing someone, of course." He raised a curious eyebrow.

"No. Since I've moved here, I haven't had much time for a dating life. Precious Moments keeps me pretty busy. However, what makes you think I want to spend time with you just because you're in town?"

His face scrunched in an amused expression. "Ouch, woman. I thought we could hang out and catch up. I haven't seen or spoken to you since the day before you moved here. Plus, the real reason why I'm here is that I need to discuss something important. Didn't want to tell you over the phone."

Her thoughts trekked back to their last night together. When she'd arrived at his home, he'd surprised her with candles lit everywhere and a trail of pink rose petals that led to his bedroom. Unlike their crazy, wild sex sessions, that last one had been more passionate and intense than all the others. For a moment, an emotional side had taken over and she'd hidden her face in his chest to suppress her tears. However, he'd noticed and kissed them away while mumbling something about how he was going to miss her, which had slammed her back to reality. Unfortunately, since she'd been away from Memphis, that night had crept into her thoughts, making her think she actually liked him for more than just great sex and conversation.

"What could we possibly have to discuss?" she asked with a slight frown.

A mischievous grin inched up his face. "Our divorce."

Zaria's beautiful face cracked into a ball of confusion, and she eyed him as if he'd just told her pigs could actually fly and were doing so that very instant. Garrett had considered calling her, but he figured it was better to tell her in person. He hadn't planned on attending the medical conference, but he figured it would be the perfect excuse to see her and to share the news that had nearly given him a heart attack.

Pulling him by the hand, she led him around the corner and found a meeting room that was unoccupied. He glanced at the digital board next to the door and noted the next session in that room was an hour and a half away.

Shutting the door, Zaria paced back and forth before stopping and settling seething eyes on him. Sighing, as he was sure he saw steam rise from her head, she invaded his personal space and her four-inch wedged sandals practically made her eye level.

"What do you mean divorce? We have to be married in order to get a divorce."

Chuckling, he lifted her chin as her breathe sucked in. "We *are* married, Mrs. Braxton," he stated matter-of-factly. "Have been for little over a year. Our one-year anniversary was two weeks ago."

"Huh?" she asked in disbelief.

"We got hitched in Vegas. Surely you remember." He paused, and a sly smirk crossed his face while he drew her against him sensually. Lowering his head, he rested his lips against hers, and they quivered at his touch. "Especially the honeymoon. I couldn't get enough of you, and you definitely couldn't get enough of me. Mmm … two whole days of ecstasy. We never left the room."

She smacked her lips and pushed against his chest, but he didn't budge.

"It was a joke, remember? We thought it would be a cool, silly thing to do since we were in Vegas. We aren't actually married, you idiot."

"Well the joke is on us. The wedding chapel called to wish us happy anniversary. I told the lady we weren't really married, and she said, 'Honey child, yes you are. You signed a marriage license.' You do remember we obtained one at the courthouse beforehand. The chapel filed it for us. Apparently it was a part of our wedding package. She faxed a copy right over. I had my attorney look at it and it's legit. We're in the system as husband and wife."

"This is crazy. Insane!" She backed away and this time he let her go. "A Michael Jackson impersonator gave me away. An Elvis Presley impersonator married us for crying out loud, and an Isley Brothers tribute band serenaded us with "For the Love of You." It wasn't even a real wedding."

"Nope, Mrs. Braxton," he started, reaching into his conference bag and handing her the folded license, "you're definitely my wife. We signed the form for a license in the state of Nevada and it was processed. Happy Anniversary, babe," he teased, hoping to ease the surprise and her anger.

Her almond-shaped eyes stretched into wide saucers as she skimmed over the paper. Shaking her head back and forth, she slammed the license on his chest. "This is unreal. I can't be married to you!" She started pacing once more before plopping into one of the leather swivel chairs at a conference table. "This can't be happening." She ran her hands through her long, straight hair and let out a bewildered sigh.

He strode over and hoisted himself on the table in front of her. "I'm not so bad once you get to know me."

"You're full of it," she said through clenched teeth.

"Why are you upset with me? Takes two to tango, sweetheart."

"So what did your lawyer say? Can we get this thing annulled? Clearly it's a mistake. Obviously we don't want to be married."

"Yeah, he mentioned an annulment," Garrett replied, casually shrugging his shoulders. "It's an easy process. Shouldn't take more than thirty to sixty days for a judge to sign off on it. Or …" He raised a cocky eyebrow.

Cutting her eyes at him, Zaria pursed her lips together. "Or what?"

"Or we can stay married."

CHAPTER TWO

Zaria repeated Garrett's ludicrous suggestion over and over in her head because surely she'd misheard the ridiculous nonsense that had spilled from his mouth. The man couldn't be serious. Being married to anyone at this moment in her life was out of the question, and being married to him was never going to happen. Sure, they were compatible in the bedroom, had similar views and interests, and they enjoyed each other's company. However, that didn't constitute a marriage.

Standing, she rested her hands on her hips and glared at him. "Why would I want to stay married to you?"

"Um ... don't you remember our agreement a few years back that if you weren't married by age thirty you'd marry me if I wasn't married or in a serious relationship? Don't you turn thirty this fall, young lady?"

She swished her lips to the side. "It was a joke, just like all of this." Snatching the paper from him, she tore it up in his hands.

"Did you do that for a dramatic effect? You know tearing it up doesn't dissolve it, right?" he asked teasingly, stuffing the pieces in his conference bag.

"Not funny, and I'm not staying married to you. Do I need to retain a lawyer, as well?"

"Why, you want half?" He started laughing.

"This shit isn't funny." Her voice raised and echoed thanks to the acoustics in the empty room. Taking a deep breath, she slammed back into the chair and glared at his amused expression.

"You know I hate when you curse," he stated. "You're too pretty for that. But I'm serious."

"You want a long-distance marriage?" she asked sarcastically, knowing full well she wasn't going to entertain his dumb proposal. "I'm not moving back to Memphis."

"Not asking you to. My college buddy, Blake Harrison, has a practice just over the bridge in Brunswick. He wants me to join him as a partner since his other primary care physician is moving to Atlanta soon. I've been contemplating it. I need a change from Memphis. And now that my wife is here, I have more reasons to move."

"You have got to be kidding me. You've actually considered this?"

"Look, I know this is shocking. Trust me, when I found out I was floored. I couldn't believe it either. But now that I've had some time to process it, I figure why not. I'm almost forty. No kids. It's time I settle down. We get along, we're both ambitious, our lovemaking is off the charts, and you can't deny that there's something between us. Always has been, darling. I saw the way your eyes roamed over me and the sinful smile that inched across your face when you saw me. You wanted me. Sure, we always do when we see each other, but there was something else there." Pausing, a knowing expression washed across his face. "I think you missed me this past year."

Garrett was right. She'd missed him, but she wasn't going to admit it. When she saw him it took everything in her not to run to him, tear off his clothes, and drag his body on top of hers. Yes, in front of all the doctors in the lobby area. Zaria hated to admit to herself that he was the only man she thought about since moving to St. Simons. She'd wondered about him and had even considered calling just to say hello. When his best friend Sean and his fiancée Traci called a few months back about their wedding plans at the end of the summer, Zaria was elated that Garrett would be one of the best men, which meant she would see him and possibly more if he was single. However, being his wife or anyone's wife for that matter wasn't on her agenda at the moment.

"Perhaps, you need glasses."

"I know you, Zaria. I've been very in tune with you physically and mentally since day one. I noticed it especially the last time I saw you. The last time we made love, and I do *mean* made love. We didn't have sex that night as you are very well aware. Sometimes I wonder did we ever have sex."

A cool shiver ran across her skin at his words. The white elephant that had been in his bedroom that night was present once more. They had indeed made love; it was sensual and emotional all wrapped into one. Nestled in his embrace, she couldn't tear herself away. However, Zaria was scared to say anything because she was leaving the next day. She couldn't get the words out that she would miss him, too.

Garrett's sudden movement startled her into a loud gasp escaping her throat. He snatched her from the chair by the waist and imprisoned his lips possessively over hers. A heated rush soared through every cell in her body as he delved his tongue deeper into her mouth and circled around hard and wicked. She clutched his shoulders for support when she found herself being hoisted up onto his body. Locking her legs tight around his waist, she returned the passionate kiss with the fervent desire that had been buried in her during the year they'd been apart. Moans filled the room, but she couldn't decipher whether they were coming from her or him. Intertwining one of his hands in her tresses, he tugged her head back, and slid his hot tongue down her neck. The hardness of him strained between her legs, and she wanted him that very instant.

"I know you missed me, baby," he growled through his teeth, placing tantalizing kisses on her skin. "I need you. Right now."

Zaria quivered at the thought of being connected with him once more and a sigh of relief rushed from her mouth. He rested his hands on either side of her face and stared at her with such a deep longing and passion that it caused her eyes to well with emotion. It was on the tip of her tongue to say she'd missed him, too. Instead, she wrestled out of his hold and backed away as confusion filled his face.

Eyeing her purse on the table, she snatched it and bolted out of the door. She heard Garrett scream out, "Wait!" She didn't know if he was following her or not as she fast-walked while rustling around in her purse for her shades which she hastily slipped on. She reached back in for her keys, but remembered she'd handed them to Patricia's assistant to retrieve the flowers from her SUV. Spotting him heading inside the conference center with her keys in tow, she rushed toward him as he began to tell her he was done. She mumbled, "Thank you," seized the keys, and continued her long strides to the parking lot without looking back to see if Garrett was behind her.

Settled in her Range Rover, she sped off toward the bridge to St. Simons Island. Her lips and insides burned from Garrett's hot tongue and hands caressing her body. Zaria didn't know which was worse—the fact that they were married and he wanted to stay that way, or the fact that she didn't realize how much she missed him until now. No, she was wrong. Who was she fooling? She'd missed him that entire year, but had it buried deep into her brain. Now it was front and center. The worst part was he knew it, and would probably use that knowledge to his advantage.

Once she returned to her beach cottage, Zaria poured herself a shot of scotch that she had on hand for when her dad would visit, and plopped on the couch. Her mind wandered back to the fact she was a married woman. She laughed out loud at the ridiculous notion that she was actually someone's wife and had been for a freaking year. Sure, settling down and having a family was on her list, far down on the list, but it had always been a goal. Her parents were happily married, and she wanted that undeniable love and best friend relationship they'd shared for thirty-five years. Though, at the same time she wanted the freedom to live her life as she saw fit, have a successful business, and not have to answer to anyone. Men were distractions, which was why she never stayed in any relationship too long. Garrett had always been her safety net. They could have sex without any expectations of going any further, for neither of them wanted a committed relationship. Except that one time he asked her how she felt about dating exclusively and she shut the conversation down with a definite no. Now he actually wanted to axe an annulment and stay married. Perhaps, he was going through a mid-life crisis.

Grabbing her cell phone, she decided to call him, but had second thoughts when he answered on the first ring.

"Changed your mind, darling?"

"Never. Are you going through a mid-life crisis? You haven't bought a motorcycle or an expensive sports car have you?" she questioned in teasing manner even though she was slightly serious.

"No. I'm not going through anything except withdrawals from being away from you."

"Whatever." She sipped her drink, hoping it would suppress the heat pooling inside of her that he'd erupted earlier. She wanted him, but she couldn't let him think he had a chance to convince her to stay married. She liked their arrangement, and if he was indeed moving to Brunswick, she wouldn't mind continuing the same agreement they'd had in Memphis.

"What are you doing on Monday?" he asked.

"Why?"

"I have an appointment with a real estate agent to look at houses over in Brunswick and on the island. Nothing set in stone. Just want to have an idea of what's on the market here. Thought perhaps you could tag along so I can get your opinion. I mean, you are my wife."

"I'm not your wife."

"According to that paper you shredded into pieces, you are."

"Look, as soon as you get back to Memphis, you have your lawyer draw up whatever paperwork so we can get this nonsense over with. Mail me the papers and I will happily sign them to terminate our so-called marriage."

He was silent, and for a moment she thought the call had dropped until she heard him sigh in a frustrated fashion.

"Fine. So we're cool?"

"Of course we are," she answered honestly. "I just won't take any more trips to Vegas with you and decide to have a spur of the moment wedding because we thought it would be fun for Elvis to marry us, forgetting to read the fine print."

"Yeah, but you have to admit we had a blast."

"Yep. It was my first time to Vegas." She paused for a moment, knowing that's not what he meant. "So you're really moving to Brunswick?"

"Yeah. After you ran off because you can't handle me anymore, I bumped into my friend whose practice I was telling you about. I'm in the car now following him to check it out."

Lifting off the couch, she trekked barefoot across the hardwood to her bedroom and laid across the bed. The events of the day had begun to give her a headache. "First of all, I can handle you just fine."

"So why did you leave? I've never known you to run from me ... well, except when I'm hitting it from the back and you can't take it anymore. Perhaps, you're finally realizing that we're meant to be. Maybe Blake asking me to move to Brunswick and our marriage is a sign we belong together. That and the fact you happened to show up at the conference center today without listening to my voicemail."

"Whatever, old man. I go over to Jekyll Island often. You believe what you want. You just make sure to see your attorney. I gotta go. I've been up since three this morning setting up for a wedding, and I have to be at the brunch early in the morning to set up for that."

"No problem. I'm flying out early Tuesday morning. Perhaps I can cook dinner for you Monday night at your place."

She almost agreed, but then remembered Brooklyn lived two cottages down. "No ... Brooklyn lives by me and is always over here. Where are you staying?"

"The Seagate Inn."

"Cool. It has a kitchen. I stayed there the first month I lived here. What time?"

"Around six?"

"That's fine. I'll bring the wine."

"Perfect. See you then, wifey," he said, chuckling.

Groaning, she turned the phone off and tossed it on the bed before he found another smart aleck remark to make. While this situation was a bump in the road, it wasn't major—just shocking and unbelievable. Luckily, it could be resolved with an annulment. However, she sensed the dynamics of their friendship had changed. Garrett wanted more now, and in a way he always had. However, when she'd first met him she was twenty-three, only a year out of college and had her whole life in front of her. Settling down and putting dreams aside for a husband and children hadn't been in her immediate future, and it still wasn't now almost seven years later. Sure she was approaching thirty, but who said one has to be married and with child at that age? Yes, her parents married fresh out of college but that was eons ago and times had changed. But no, staying married to Garrett was out of the question; however, if he was serious about moving to the St. Simons/Brunswick area than at least her drought would end.

Reagan glided out onto the veranda overlooking the pristine blue and green Atlantic Ocean. She placed a pitcher of mimosas on the table next to the vegetable omelets and pecan waffles, along with the shrimp and grits she'd made for Precious Moments Events' weekly Monday brunch meeting at her home, which also served as their place of business.

Zaria greeted her with a smile and a long, satisfied moan. "Everything is delish, girl. Your brother is not the only chef in the family," she complimented, referring to Reagan's big brother Justin Richardson who owned a popular blues and dinner club on Beale Street in Memphis. "Reminds me of home."

A beaming grin flashed across Reagan's face as she poured the champagne cocktail into the flutes on the table. "Thank you. I wanted everything perfect today."

"You sure are in a chipper mood." Zaria slid one of the glasses and placed it next to her loaded plate. "Champagne at eleven on a Monday morning? What are we celebrating?"

Sitting, Reagan grabbed a glass, followed by their best friend, Brooklyn Vincent. "I'm happy to say that we are booked this summer as well as into the fall and winter months with more weddings and events than I ever imagined."

"Oh that's wonderful news, indeed," Brooklyn answered, as the ladies clinked their glasses together. "Cheers and here's to many, many more busy and prosperous years together."

"Well, I couldn't have done it without the two of you uprooting your lives last summer and moving from Memphis to help me." Reagan paused, wiping a few tears away. "You just don't know how much that means to me. To move here on a whim after doing a few destination weddings, I know was insane, but I was tired of working for someone else. It just felt right, you know? When you feel like something is for you, you have to go after it. Pursuing my dream of owning an event planning company wasn't going to happen if I didn't make it happen. And I know everyone questioned why St. Simons, but I love the slow-paced and peaceful surroundings way better than the fast-paced life and hustle and bustle I experienced in Atlanta. I'm just glad everything panned out the way it did."

Zaria smiled at her cousin. "We've joked about it for years, and it just seemed like the perfect time to take the plunge."

"Well, I'm glad you did because business is wonderful. I think perhaps we should start searching for another event planner. What do you ladies, think?"

Brooklyn, the accountant and photographer, nodded her head in agreement. "We definitely need the extra help, and we can afford another salary position. What do you think, Zaria?"

Sipping her drink, Zaria drew her attention back into the meeting. While she was excited for their success, her thoughts still lingered on the news that had rattled her since Saturday. She didn't even know why it bothered her so much in the first place. They were going to have the marriage annulled, and then it would be the end. Yet, for some reason the idea made her heart tighten, as if she was losing a real husband. And Reagan's comment of 'It just felt right, you know? When you feel like something is for you, you have to go after it' sounded loud in Zaria's ears. It made her think of Garrett the instant Reagan said it which was weird, but Zaria could imagine him saying it about them. The thought was crazy, and she laughed it off in her head.

"I think that's a wonderful idea. We could use the extra help."

"Splendid. We can start the search this week. I have a few people in mind." Reagan's eyes perused over the notepad next to her plate before settling on Zaria. "Are you okay?"

"Oh, yes. Just a little tired from this long weekend." It wasn't a lie for she hadn't been able to sleep thanks to Garrett's announcement, but she couldn't tell her cousin and best friend because they had no idea about her off and on rendezvous for the past six years. Everyone in their circle assumed she despised him while Garrett, on the other hand, always made it clear he found her irresistible. Zaria wanted to confess, especially now with her mixed emotions over him, but she didn't know how she could form her lips to say, "Hey, I'm married to what's-his-face, but we're getting a divorce." No, she couldn't spring that on them even though she needed to get it off her chest.

"Yes, it was a long weekend and we're each taking on more responsibilities, which is why we need to hire another planner. On another note, I spoke to Sean and he said Traci is fretting over the wedding details. Since all the events are at the Memphis Botanical Gardens because she's a botanist there, their event planners are taking care the wedding and reception; however, we agreed to assist with everything else and we have from afar, but the bride is becoming nervous with the wedding less than two months away. That's understandable. One of us needs to go to Memphis soon to see what needs to be done to tie up any loose strings and to relax her jitters." Reagan turned to Zaria. "Since you aren't scheduled to work the event next weekend, can you go for a few days?"

Zaria looked forward to that time off, but she didn't want the bride feeling overwhelmed. Plus, she hadn't seen her parents in three months. "Of course. I'll call her this afternoon."

"Perfect." She clapped her manicured hands together. "Well, that's all the business I have for today. Let's enjoy our meal and then get back to work."

After brunch, Zaria headed to the Pier Village to meet with a client to finalize plans for an upcoming garden club fundraiser event. However, all she could think about was the fact that she was married. The sooner they got this charade over the better—before she started to think that Dr. Garrett Braxton could be the one.

CHAPTER THREE

Setting the cornbread on the counter, a pleased smile crossed Garrett's face when the doorbell rung on time, just as he expected it would. Zaria was a stickler for punctuality. Tossing the oven mitt next to the cast iron skillet, he rushed to the foyer as the bell chimed again. She was also impatient. Opening the door, he met her smoldering brown eyes and a faint, nervous smile that she tried to stifle. Zaria was breathtaking as always, but ever since he found out she was his wife, he saw her in a different light. The protective side that was reserved only for his sister and mother now included Zaria. Perhaps it always had.

"Don't you look stunning." Garrett stared down at Zaria, who held a bottle of Merlot in one hand and a tote bag in the other. "I'm a lucky man." He winked and stepped back.

"Just until the annulment goes through," she answered in a sing-song voice.

She handed him both items and passed through while his eyes scanned over her body and landed on the cutest butt he'd ever had the pleasure of clutching. She was casual tonight in a sexy short, off-the-shoulder white dress and flat, pink gladiator sandals, reminding him that he was taller than her. She usually preferred four to six inch heels which made her the same height as him. He watched her in silence as she sauntered inside with a sexy dip in her hips. Her hair sat in a huge bun on the top of her head, bringing out her alluring cheek bones and her inquisitive eyes as she turned and glanced at him over her shoulder.

"Whatever you're cooking smells delish." She made a sharp left into the small galley kitchen that was appointed with all the modern kitchen staples—such as stainless steel appliances, antique white cabinets, and black granite countertops.

Glancing at the cornbread, Zaria opened the pot on the stove. "Mmm … collard greens … and barbeque?" she asked with a wicked grin. Lifting the foil from the pan which held ribs, her adorable pert nose wrinkled with pleasure followed by a wink. "I could get used to this."

"Oh really?" he asked with a slight raise of his eyebrows.

She swished her lips to the side. "It's a joke, but I forgot you knew how to cook."

Setting her tote bag and wine on the counter next to the refrigerator, he wrapped his arms around her waist and drew her close to him. She tensed, but didn't pull away. Instead, she rested her backside firmly against his chest.

"I wanted to give you a taste of Memphis … and I do mean all of what I know you've missed." Traveling his tongue along the right side of her neck, she released a pleased moan. Perhaps they were falling back into their normal routine when alone. He just hoped he could convince her that they should stay married. "I know you miss home."

Stirring the greens, she nodded. "I do sometimes, more so my family, but life on the island is relaxing. It's very quiet and peaceful here. Even though I'm busy with work, my world is simple and uncomplicated … well, until you sprung your exciting news. And I say that with the upmost sarcasm." She laughed. "I'm hungry. Is everything done? I brought lettuce, spinach, and what not to make a salad."

"Cool. I just need to fry the Georgia Atlantic shrimp. They're all I've had at every restaurant since I've been here. I wanted one last batch. Too bad I can't take them back with me on the plane."

Zaria unlocked herself from his embrace and stepped over to the counter beside her. She began to pull vegetables out of the bag. "They are delicious, but I guess if you move here, you can eat them all the time." She darted her eyes at him for a quick second, and then back to chopping a cucumber. "That's one of the perks of living here. Fresh seafood whenever I want it and at reasonable prices."

"Yep, Brunswick is on the list." He dropped the shrimp in the fryer. "I have a few other offers as well, including one in Atlanta, but I did like Blake's practice and the staff. Plus, some of the homes I saw today were really nice. My favorite was a short distance away from the Pier Village. I could walk or drive a golf cart according to my real estate agent. I see why you like it here. Its quaint and everyone is friendly. Yeah, this is definitely on the list."

"Oh … good." Clearing her throat, she shook up a bottle of raspberry salad dressing and proceeded to coat the salad.

He noted the high pitch of her voice. Zaria rarely became unhinged, but she seemed off-balance as her eye contact continued to dart away from his. She was always confident and in control; however, she was acting like a nervous teenage girl around him not the sassy, witty diva he knew. He figured she was still shaken by the news he'd bestowed on her earlier.

After preparing their plates, they headed to the living room area instead of eating at the dining table. Sitting on the couch next to her, he set his wine glass and plate on the coffee table in front on them and grabbed the remote.

"Sports or news?" he asked, pointing the remote toward the flat screen television on the wall. Watching their favorite shows had always been one of their activities to do together since she refused to go out in public with him for the fear of running into someone they knew. The only time they weren't stuck in his house was when he'd invite her to go out of town with him.

"I believe "Sports Fanatic" will be on soon." She glanced at her watch. "Can't miss Rasheed Vincent giving his two cents on today's golf highlights. I'm sure Brooklyn is preparing to watch her big brother now."

"Yeah, he's a hoot. Still can't believe he and Bria are married with two children. Their relationship kind of reminds me of us."

Shooting him a questionable stare, she stuck her fork straight up in the collard greens and pursed her lips together with a pop. "How so?"

"Well ... no one knew they were seeing each other, and then all of a sudden I received an invite to their engagement party and you were planning a wedding. You and I have managed to go under the radar for six years."

"Because we're just sex buddies … well, I guess we are friends, too. I mean, I do consider you one of my best friends. Um … kind of. You know just as much about me as they do, maybe even more." She winced and placed her eyes back on the show. "They were best friends who started a relationship on the low. It was bound to happen for them to fall in love."

"Really?" He raised an amused eyebrow as he noted her unusual stammering. "I'll keep that in mind."

She smacked lips and sipped her wine. "Whatever. You just make sure to see your attorney. I'll be in Memphis next week to meet with Sean and Traci to go over their wedding plans. Have the annulment paperwork ready."

"Glad you're coming. Sean says Traci is a nervous wreck. I've been planning the bachelor party. You know, going to the strip clubs and um … making some selections."

He caught her stern glare on him out of the corner of his eye.

"Oh, you still go to the strip clubs?" she asked in a firm manner.

Was her voice laced with a tinge of jealously? He snickered and turned his head toward her. She was fully aware of him and his best friend's strip club days, which pretty much ended last spring when Sean met the love of his life. Garrett had only gone twice since Zaria moved—that lifestyle had become boring and tedious. Now he wanted more. He wanted her.

"Mad, baby?"

"Boy, please. I couldn't care less. I just think you're a little too old to still frequent the clubs."

"And I agree with you wholeheartedly. I'm so over all of the skirt-chasing and meaningless relationships as well. In fact, I have been for quite some time."

"Why isn't Cannon assisting you with the planning of the bachelor party? He's the other best man and Sean's big brother."

"He's out of the country at the moment on a Doctors Unlimited assignment, and I volunteered to handle it since I'm the only single man in the wedding party in the city ... well, technically I'm married." He winked and bit into a tender rib.

Groaning, she sipped her wine. "Not for long, Doc. You'll be single before Sean's stripper-infested party."

He simply nodded. "So, how's dinner?"

"It's perfect. You definitely put your foot in it like my grandmother says. These ribs are falling off the bone. Reminds me of Rendezvous. I have to eat there when I return home, as well as Lillian's, of course."

"Good. I'm glad it's to your liking. You can put that on the pro side of 'the reasons why I should stay married to Garrett' chart. Along with he's intelligent, quite handsome, charming, and the best lover I ever."

"Ha! You wish, old man."

"Um ... no. You've said it plenty of times, young lady. When you met me, you'd only been with inexperienced *boys* your age. You said I was the first real man you'd ever been with. The only man that had *ever* elicited multiple orgasms and put you in positions you didn't know even existed. If I remember correctly, you did most of the calling at midnight that first year of our escapade. And I saw that cat you were dating a few years ago at Bria and Rasheed's wedding. I know that dude wasn't blowing your back out or making you climb the wall all night like I was, considering you couldn't keep your eyes off of me the entire time." Standing, he swiped his empty plate from the coffee table and headed to the kitchen to scoop up the shrimp that were cooling on a paper towel. "Heck, probably why you dumped him soon-after and called me. Luckily, I'd just broken up with someone as well." He rejoined her on the couch. She'd been pretty quiet. In fact, he was surprised she hadn't interrupted him, but she knew he was telling the truth.

"Whatever, old man. And my chart is full of cons."

She snatched a few shrimp from his plate. He hated someone eating off of his plate, which she was fully aware of, but Zaria always did so to spite him. In a way, he never minded and he'd tossed a few extra shrimp on it for her.

"Oh … so there *is* a chart?" He raised an eyebrow and a cocky smirk lined his face.

She chuckled nervously. "No … I was being sarcastic. I haven't given it a second thought." Shrugging, she popped the shrimp into her mouth and walked away with her empty wine glass. "You have a chart?" she asked quietly, pouring another glass of wine and resting her chestnut eyes on him.

"It's not written down, but I've made some mental notes."

"Huh, huh. I see. What could possibly be on the con side about me?" she asked as if she was perfect.

"You really want to know?"

"Well, I am slightly curious." Setting the glass on the counter, she folded her arms across her chest and raised an inquisitive eyebrow.

Standing, he dashed toward her and yanked Zaria to him, causing a surprised gasp to emerge and her dress to slip a tad off of her soft, mocha shoulders. She stared questionably as her ample breasts—that he craved to taste—rose up and down against his chest. Her hardened nipples pierced through his shirt and her parted mouth, along with her hazy glare, signaled they were in the same mind frame. Pulling her so close that even a thin sheet of paper couldn't be edged between them, he made sure that she could feel the strain that had emerged against his pants. A sexy smirk crossed her knowing, lovely face as she realized he wanted her. No, needed her.

Garrett lowered his lips onto her succulent ones, and she clutched his sides while her breathing increased. Her pounding heart was the only sound in the quietness that surrounded them. As her breath exhaled like a cool breeze, her eyes fluttered shut for a moment, and reopened doe-wide with full contact for the first time that evening.

"What's on the con side?" she whispered with a sparkle in her eyes.

"Nothing. Absolutely-freaking nothing. You're perfect in every way, Zaria. Perfect for me."

Zaria didn't know what the hell had charged through her when Garrett stated so seriously—and almost lovingly—that she was perfect … perfect for him. Her heart stopped beating before it sped up again with a rapid hammering against her chest. She could hear it and figured he could as well. Normally, men saying such things were absurd to her and she chalked it up to them wanting to have sex, nothing more. But the endearing and heartfelt way Garrett said it, she knew he meant it.

Yearning to have his lips all the way on her, she closed the tiny gap between their mouths. She aimed to kiss him hard and deep, but he cupped her chin and bestowed gentle, sweet kisses on her that sent a warm passion to ripple through her and reach the core that made her a woman. A meek gasp sounded from Zaria as he continued with slow, tender kisses similar to the ones that she'd daydreamed about since their last time together.

Reaching his hand up to the hair band that secured her huge bun, he unwrapped it until all of her tresses fell down to her waist.

"You know I prefer your weave down," he joked, tugging gently on her hair.

Smacking her lips, she pinched his forearm playfully. "You know damn well I don't have a weave." It had been a long-running joke between them since their first tryst, when he'd pulled her hair and then stopped, citing he didn't want to pull out any tracks. She'd given him an icy stare and stated with a firm voice it was all hers.

Chuckling, he reached under her dress and snatched her panties down until they fell to the floor. "I just like the sexy way you look when you have a diva attitude moment. I missed that."

Intertwining his hands into her thick mane, he lowered his lips once more to her trembling ones and backed them up until they were at the couch, his tender kisses never ceasing. She tried to speed up, but he was in full control of her mouth, causing her mixed emotions to surface once more as an electric current raced through her blood.

Picking her up, he laid her on the couch and positioned his body on top. Drawing her legs around his waist, he hovered his mouth over hers before imprisoning her lips with the deep, fast kisses she wanted. A relieved sigh emerged. She didn't know how much more of his sweet kisses she could handle. It had begun to remind her of the last time they'd made love. She couldn't let her guard down … she couldn't fall for him.

However, she didn't want him to stop, either; she wrapped her hands around his neck and frantically returned his untamed kisses. Running his hand down her side, he tugged the hem of her dress up to her waist and reached back down past her stomach until his hand massaged her center. An intense moan erupted from her throat when one his fingers eased inside of her, darting in out. His lips left hers and trailed to her neck, causing her moans to increase while his hot tongue glided along her skin and inched down to her breasts.

"You purposely didn't wear a bra?" he whispered, clutching a nipple in between his teeth.

"Stop talking." She pushed his head deeper into her chest as his mouth engulfed the entire nipple. His hand kneaded the other breast before licking over to it and driving her insane. Her hips rotated up and an exaggerated groan sounded from her throat when he inserted another finger.

"Is that what you wanted, baby?" Resting his forehead on hers, his commanding stare and deep voice shook her as he continued jamming in and out of her so fast she found herself slipping from the couch, but he held her firm. Grasping his shoulders hard, it seemed like she was going in out of consciousness as the rush of an orgasm jetted through her body.

"Garrett ... uh ... Garrett ... please ... goodness ... Gar ..." she breathlessly screamed out over and over, yet he wouldn't let up. Her legs weakened and slid from around his waist, spreading out on the cushions until her body fell off the couch with him. But he didn't stop, it was as if he hadn't noticed. His aggressive stare focused on her face.

"Love hearing you pant my name. I missed you, woman," he growled. "Missed you more than I thought I would."

Lifting her up to him, he shifted them on the floor with his back to the couch and her straddling his lap. He continued driving her crazy with wild, passion-filled kisses that awakened pleasure within her. Zaria wanted him. Craved him. Needed to feel him pulse inside of her until her voice was hoarse from screaming his name. She'd missed him as well. Missed all the naughty things they used to do, but she also missed *him*. Missed his laughter, his compassionate nature, and the way he would gaze at her as if she was the only woman in the world to him. She missed their in-depth conversations, their quiet, lazy afternoons watching football or old movies, and even their petty arguments because they usually ended with them in an acrobatic position joined together.

Garrett's lips left hers and reclaimed her breasts once more as he leaned her back onto the floor. Grasping her butt cheeks, he traveled his tongue down until it reached where his fingers were and he licked her with light strokes over and over, causing her legs to shake. It tickled until he delved deeper and her giggles turned into fervent moans. Holding onto his head, her hips rotated against his mouth at the same pace and amorous sounds filled the air.

"That feels so good, G. Don't you ever stop." She glanced down at him to see his tongue kissing her other lips just as he'd kissed her mouth earlier. "Damn, baby."

"I don't plan on stopping. You have me forever. I thought you realized that by now."

"Hush all the marriage nonsense, old man, and just keep doing what you're doing with that lethal tongue."

"I intend to make love to you all night."

With that comment, her thoughts trekked back to their last night together and the sweet, sensual love they made.

"We can't make love. We don't love each other, but you can fuck me however you want, G."

Stopping, he sat up and picked her up from the floor, setting her firmly back on the couch. He remained standing in front of her with a bewildered expression on his face.

"What's wrong?" she asked. "You don't have any condoms?" She pulled her dress down and straightened the top of it back over her breasts. She had a strict no condoms, no sex rule.

"Uh … yes, but that's not why I stopped." A sincere, loving expression washed over his features as he sat next to her and grabbed her hands. Exhaling, he gave her his full attention. "Zaria, I'm serious about us. I know you think I'm insane for saying it, but I honestly believe it was fate we are in fact married."

Yes, I do believe you're insane for thinking we should stay married. "Garrett …"

"I'm in love with you, Zaria," he said sincerely, placing a tender hand on her cheek. "I have been since the moment I laid eyes on you."

Zaria's body quivered with cold fear as she repeated his words in her head. She knew he adored her. She knew he cared about her and liked her more than he should, which was always why she kept him a bay.

"G, you can't possibly be in love with me … I … I mean …"

"Wait, babe. Just hear me out. I remember when I first met you. Justin was doing the catering for the scholarship fundraiser and wanted me to meet with you to go over details. Honestly, I don't know what I was expecting but when you strutted into the Cultural Arts Center like you owned the place my first thought was damn she's fine. You wore a sexy but classy straight red dress and matching pumps showcasing those long, mocha legs. Your hair tumbled in curls down your back and your lips … mmm, those kissable, pouty lips that I yearned to have on me … *wherever* on me. And while my first thoughts were lustful, it all changed when you smiled, held out your hand and introduced yourself, and commenced to telling me your ideas for the event. You were in control of yourself and your surroundings. You were intelligent, witty, and quite mature for only twenty-three years old. I couldn't get you off my mind for the rest of the week. And the more we met and chatted on the phone to discuss the fundraiser, I found myself smitten over you which was new for me. Sure, I've had girlfriends and found women attractive, but with you it was different. And even though you've kept me at arm's length and have this guard over your heart, I've still fallen for you. Fallen hard, woman, and I know you have those same feelings. I realized it that night before you left Memphis. You cried while we made love. I knew then that I loved you, and it took everything in me to not ask you to stay in Memphis with me. But at the same time, I wanted you to follow your dreams. I figured if we were truly meant to be then it would happen. When I received the phone call from the wedding chapel I knew it was fate."

Zaria stared at him dumbfounded as she processed everything he'd said. She was flattered and terrified at the same time. She definitely had deep feelings for him, but the whole marriage thing was just too much and moving way too fast for her.

Her breathing became unhinged and goose bumps prickled along her skin as she stood and faced him.

"Garrett, we won't work. I'm not ready to be someone's devoted, loving wife. Please just let this go," she shouted louder than she intended to.

"So you feel nothing for me?"

"I didn't say that but this is all so sudden. You've basically just come out of nowhere and told me we've been married for a year, you're contemplating moving here, and you're supposedly in love with me. I'm not ready for any of this. I just want to live my life without any distractions and complications, make Precious Moments Events the best and most sought-after event planning company in the area, and be happy. Which I am, and being married to you or anyone else for that matter is not in my plans. We can't do this anymore. I'm done."

Walking away from him, she eyed her purse on the kitchen counter, grabbed it, and headed toward the door with him on her heel. His hand grabbed her forearm, and he turned her around to face him.

"Tell me you don't love me, and I'll leave you alone."

Wrestling out of his embrace, she pivoted on her heel and opened the door but he reached over her head and pushed it hard. She thought for sure the door would fall off the hinges.

Wrapping one arm around her waist, he leaned his head down to her ear. "You didn't answer me," he reminded, through clenched teeth.

Without turning to face him, she broke his hold, opened the door, and fled out of the condo directly down the hallway to the elevator, the tears flowing freely down her cheeks. Zaria hated not to answer him, but the truth was she couldn't because of what she feared she would say. And once she said it, she couldn't take it back.

CHAPTER FOUR

"I'm so glad you're here!" Traci Reed exclaimed in relief, giving Zaria an affectionate hug when she entered Traci's office at the Memphis Botanical Gardens. "I've been a nervous wreck, but having you here makes me feel so much better. I keep joking to everyone that Sean and I should jet to Las Vegas and elope, but my mother would kill me." She giggled, and her bouncy ponytail flung back and forth. "Have a seat." Motioning to the chair in front of her desk, Traci headed around to sit in hers.

At the mention of Vegas, Zaria's chest tightened, reminding her that she was still a married woman. She hadn't spoken or communicated with Garrett since she'd dashed out of his condo last week like Flo Jo. He'd called and sent text messages, but she hadn't returned any of them and had no plans to— even though at night her dreams were haunted with weird nightmares. In one he wore a tuxedo and was kissing her passionately while whispering how much he loved her. She woke up with tears streaming down her cheeks. In another one, she was running toward him in a field of purple flowers with her arms spread wide, hair blowing carefree in the wind, and laughing hysterically as if she was elated to see him. Last night's dream was the worst. They were remarrying, except this time it was the fantasy wedding she'd planned ever since she was a little girl—the white horse with a pink and gold carriage; a harpist playing "The Wedding March" and everyone dressed in black and white. As she glided down the aisle toward a smiling Garrett, Zaria shook herself awake and refused to go back to sleep for the fear of finishing the dream.

Crossing her legs, Zaria grabbed her notepad and pen from her tote bag. "Yes, your mother would be devastated if you eloped. Besides, I'm here now to help you with your concerns," she said with a comforting smile.

"I appreciate it. My biggest dilemma is dealing with my maid of honor and my matron of honor. They don't get along for whatever reasons. They're bickering over the planning of my bachelorette party and my shower."

Stunned, Zaria tilted her head to the side. "How do you know they're arguing? You shouldn't be in the planning process."

"I'm not. They keep calling me complaining about the other. They've never gotten along. Or rather my cousin Stacy has never gotten along with Caitlyn, but she's my best friend. More than that, she's like a sister to me because I'm an only child. I keep telling them they have to work together and leave me out of it. I have enough on my plate to worry about."

At the mention of the maid of honor, Caitlyn Clarke, Zaria groaned in her head while still nodding and listening to Traci continue to ramble and rant about the two frenemies. She didn't have anything against Caitlyn, but rather what happened that made her realize she had feelings for Garrett that she couldn't suppress.

Zaria remembered the evening like it was yesterday when Garrett and Sean strolled into Lillian's Blues and Dinner Club last spring when she was still the event coordinator there. They'd beelined it straight to Traci and Caitlyn's table, and Garrett seemed quite smitten with the flirtatious, pretty woman. They'd danced and chatted most of the night, and left together hand-in-hand. Normally, Zaria wouldn't be jealous but she was and hated it. However, at around one o'clock that morning, he'd called saying he'd hung out with Caitlyn but nothing happened. They'd just watched movies and talked about how Sean and Traci were falling for each other. She'd questioned his need to explain himself to her because it wasn't necessary. They were sex buddies, nothing more. Even though deep down Zaria was fuming, especially when he stated he didn't want her to be hurt. She hated to admit that for some reason she was, but played it off and told him she didn't care what he did. Two weeks later they were in Vegas for a medical conference and married each other for the fun of it. She moved to St. Simons soon after with a heavy heart because she discovered that the mixed emotions over him weren't mixed at all, but she pushed them aside and concentrated on her new business venture.

"I'll meet with both ladies and get this mess straightened out. From now on, they need to call me not you. You can't be stressed out. What else?"

"The final fittings are tomorrow for the bridesmaids, but I'm not able to go because of work obligations. Tomorrow is the opening of a new summer garden, and I have to be here since I'm the head designer of it."

"No problem. That's why I'm here. I'll be happy to go to the fittings."

"Perfect. Sean is making his final selections for the tuxedos an hour before, so if you could peep in on him for me that would be awesome. It's in the same location. I believe Garrett and some of the other men will be there as well."

"Of course." Zaria's right hand trembled as she jotted down the information. The plan while in Memphis was to not see Garrett. She didn't want to hear from him until he had the necessary paperwork she needed to sign to end their sham-of-a-marriage. Even then she didn't want to see him and figured she could stop by the attorney's office to sign the papers.

After writing down more tasks to ease the bride's mind, she left so Traci could finish a project in the rose topiaries. Zaria met with the event planning division of the gardens, who was handling the ceremony setup which was to take place in the rose gardens and the reception that would be held under a nearby tent. However, she was responsible for the bridal party bouquets and Reagan was responsible for the wedding procession. They hated not being more involved, but Sean stated that he wanted family and friends to enjoy his wedding day and not worry about the hassle of working. However, Justin was holding the rehearsal dinner at Lillian's as a gift from him and Shelbi.

On the way to Lillian's for an early dinner with the Arrington sisters, Zaria made the necessary phone calls, including a three-way call to Caitlyn and Stacy to make them understand that they were to leave the bride out of their bickering. She also decided that instead of them working on both events together, they should each work on one. Caitlyn was given the shower along with Sean's three sisters who were bridesmaids, and Stacy the bachelorette party with the other two bridesmaids who were cousins of the bride.

Taking a deep sigh, Zaria entered the restaurant and her eyes immediately landed on her cousin-in-law, Shelbi Arrington-Richardson, who was in the waiting area. A warm smile crossed her glowing, honeyed-coated face and her healthy curls bounced around her shoulders when she strolled over.

"Hey, Z," she squealed out, giving Zaria a big squeeze. "I can't believe it's been a year since we've seen each other. You look beautiful as always, diva. Justin and I miss you at the restaurant, but we understand pursuing your dreams."

"I miss you guys as well but I am enjoying my career move."

Zaria pulled back for she didn't want to smash Shelbi, and glanced down at the little baby bump that protruded slightly from her pink maxi dress. "Hello, you two." Zaria winked and blew a kiss at Shelbi's stomach. Linking arms, they trekked into the dining area of the restaurant. They settled at a table far away from the stage so the music from the blues band wouldn't drown out their conversation. The restaurant was halfway full, but it would be packed after five o' clock. It always was on the Wind Down Wednesday's Happy Hour night. It had been one of her suggestions during the restaurant's first year when Justin stated that business was slow on Wednesday nights.

"How are you feeling today?" Zaria asked. The last time she spoke to Shelbi she hung up in a hurry to throw-up her lunch.

"Much better now that I'm out of my first trimester. Hungry all the time, but luckily my husband is a chef. My sisters should be here soon. Raven is at the hospital delivering a baby and Bria just left the practice. She had an acupuncture session that ran over."

"Can't wait to see them. I miss hanging with the Arrington clan."

Once seated, Zaria perused over the menu she knew by heart even though there were a few additions. She decided on Justin's signature seafood gumbo with a chicken and pecan spinach salad, which was a new item on the menu. Glancing at a waiter carrying rib entrées, her thoughts drifted to Garrett's mouth-watering ribs ... and somehow on his lips placing tantalizing kisses on her body and the intense way he gazed at her as if she belonged to him. Shaking her head, she needed to erase all emotions and feelings for him. It was over and that was all there was to it. Besides, they wouldn't work anyway. On the plane, she'd typed a pros and cons list on her cell phone just for the heck of it, and even though there weren't any cons, she wasn't ready to be married.

A waitress she wasn't familiar with jotted down their orders and since Shelbi knew what her sisters wanted, she placed theirs as well.

"Hello, ladies," Raven Arrington-Phillips greeted as she approached the table along with her sister Bria Arrington-Vincent with hugs and laughs.

Plopping into her chair, Bria slid her sunglasses on her head. "So glad you came to check on our brother and Traci."

"Me too. I just left a meeting with the blushing bride, as well as diffused the situation with her maid and matron of honor. No one has time for their pettiness."

"Yeah, they have been a thorn in her side," Bria admitted. "I thought they were going to curse each other out at our first gown fitting. I hope everything goes well tomorrow."

"Oh it will or I'll be there cursing them out if they don't get their acts together. I spoke to both of them earlier, and they agreed to be cordial for Traci's sake. I divvied up the tasks, and since you all know Caityln I figured you could help her with the shower."

Raven nodded her head. "No problem. We told Stacy she could have it at the Arrington Estate when we met for a wedding meeting a few months back with Reagan. Mother definitely doesn't mind. But Stacy never called me back, and when I called Caitlyn she said Stacy wanted to handle the venues. I'll contact Cait later on this evening."

"Thank you. I appreciate it."

"We just want everything perfect for Sean's wedding," Raven said sincerely. "We never thought in a million years he'd meet a woman that he'd fall in love with and marry. And what makes it so wonderful is that she's the total opposite of the model, superficial-type he only dated for years.

Traci is such a quirky and intelligent sweetheart. It's cool she turned out to be his kind of girl after all, and we love her so much."

"Can't believe all the Arringtons will be married, and I've planned all of your weddings ... well, except for Cannon and Yasmine."

Bria laughed. "Well ... those two wanted to be married ASAP after spending over a decade apart. I don't blame them for jetting off to Vegas and eloping." Tapping her chin, Bria pondered on something. "You know, that would be kind of cool for a spur-of-the-moment vows renewal. Just me, Rasheed, and an Elvis Presley impersonator officiating the ceremony, of course. Wouldn't that be fun?" she chuckled.

"Loads of it!" Zaria laughed a little too loud. *You can go to the same place I did*, Zaria added sarcastically in her head. *You'll have your choice of Michael Jackson or Prince giving you away.*

The waitress arrived with their food and the ladies commenced eating, but Zaria found herself swirling her gumbo around in the bowl. It was the second time that day someone mentioned eloping in Vegas for the fun of it. She wanted to burst out with, 'That's what Garrett and I did and we've been married for a whole year and didn't even freaking know it. Not only that, my husband wants to move to where I am, stay married, and have babies because he thinks he's in love with me and has been since the moment he laid eyes on me. Okay, so who can blame him for that? Yet I did nothing to lead him on and make him think we were more than just sex buddies. I mean, sure we have fun, travel, and share things with each other that we wouldn't dare share with anyone else, but everyone needs that one confidant to confide in that can be trusted. Sometimes you can't tell your family and girlfriends your deepest fears, regrets, and dreams. Right?'

Zaria was going insane on the inside because she had no one to share it with. But it was her decision to keep it a secret. During the course of their relationship, she needed to confide in Reagan and Brooklyn but couldn't spill the words out. And she wasn't even sure why she kept going over and over it in her head. However, the fact that he was in love with her wreaked havoc on her heart and she couldn't jolt it out of her thought process. Luckily, she realized that Shelbi was speaking to her and was grateful for the interruption.

"Zaria, I know you have a love/hate relationship with Garrett, but he was just on Jekyll Island for a conference. He's considering moving to the area."

Taking a sip of her margarita, Zaria was no longer grateful for the interruption. Shelbi was always good at mentioning him. For some reason she thought they belonged together. "Mmm ... well, I'm sure he'll find a job," she answered nonchalantly as she always did when he was mentioned. "There are plenty of hospitals and private practices in the area."

"Oh, but he has," Shelbi answered in an upbeat, cheerful manner. "Sean had a cookout this weekend, and Garrett announced that he'd taken a position with our friend from medical school. He's preparing to move down there in about month or so. In fact, he called his real estate agent about a house he loved the on the main island. So it's a done deal." Shelbi paused, showcasing a mischievous grin. "I guess the man you love to hate will be on the same tiny island with you. Can't escape Garrett, huh?"

Zaria's heart dropped down to her red manicured toes and beads of perspiration formed on the back of her neck. She'd hoped he would take the position in Atlanta since she never answered his question and she was adamant about not staying married. Being on the same tiny island, as Shelbi mentioned, would be utter torture.

Clearing her throat, Zaria turned on her usual I-don't-give-a-damn-about-Garrett façade. "Girl, nobody is thinking about him. He can live wherever. It doesn't mean I have to see him. And if I do, I'm always cordial to the man. He's simply not my cup of tea."

"Perhaps its fate," Shelbi suggested.

"Please. There is nothing I want with Dr. Braxton, but I wish him success."

They ate and continued catching up while listening to the blues band. The sisters did most of the talking, mostly about the wedding and Shelbi's pregnancy, while Zaria pretended to listen as numbness took over her body. After an hour Raven dashed off when she received a message that one of her patients was being rushed to hospital and Bria left to relieve the nanny of her duties.

"So are you dating anyone?" Shelbi asked, biting into a crab cake.

"No time with events back to back, but we're not complaining at all. How do you like finally working at Arrington Family Specialists with your family?"

"It's wonderful. I'm glad I made the decision to finish my residency, but Justin lets me create dishes for the menu and help with catering events if I have time so I'm living both my dreams. Well, now another one," she beamed, patting her stomach. "Sooooo, do you think you'll ever settle down and get married? I remember that one guy you dated um … Kelsey Drake, the attorney. Seemed kind of serious to me."

Zaria had forgotten all about Kelsey. Nice guy, but he never quite did it for her. She wasn't sure why she dated him in the first place. He wasn't charming or affectionate, and he was terrible in bed. No emotions. No foreplay. No orgasm. No nothing. When he'd asked her to marry him she nearly laughed out loud because she had no idea why he'd even asked. She'd never told him she loved him and hadn't given any inclination that she wanted forever with him.

"Nope, at least not for me. Just not my cup of tea."

"Huh, huh." The mischievous grin appeared on Shelbi's face. "Or maybe you've been waiting for Garrett."

Zaria's forehead crunched with confusion. "And why would I wait for him?"

Shelbi leaned in and whispered, "Can I tell you a secret?"

"Sure." Zaria said it calmly but her pulse began to race.

"I know you two hooked up."

"He told you?" she screamed a little too loud and patrons from a nearby table glanced her way. She smiled and nodded at them before leaning over the table to Shelbi, and with clenched teeth asked, "What did he say?"

"No ... no one has told me anything. I overheard you one time in your office. It was late. The restaurant had just closed, but I was next door in Justin's office trying to sleep between shifts at the hospital. Garrett was asking you about taking your relationship to another level and you told him you liked the way things were. Of course this was after you two had sex. Very loud, passionate sex."

Zaria sat back in her chair and exhaled to calm her pounding heart down. No wonder Shelbi always mentioned him; she'd known all along. Zaria remembered that evening, too. Garrett was hanging at Lillian's with his boys, and he'd gazed at her with hungry eyes the entire time as if he wanted to devour her. She'd sent him a text message to meet her in her office. Justin was in the kitchen so she assumed his office next door was empty. They'd had sex the moment Garrett entered on the wall that was shared with Justin's office. *Damn it!*

"Did you tell your husband?"

Shelbi smiled sympathetically. "No. I haven't told a single soul. I'd hoped eventually you two would come out it with it. I've seen the way he stares at you. Heck, at my wedding reception I could've sworn you gave him a haughty look and he raised a sexy eyebrow as if he knew what it meant. When he said he was moving to Brunswick, I prayed it was because of you. I thought perhaps the distance away from each other had convinced you two that you were soul mates."

"Well, our relationship is over. If you want to call it a real relationship. We just hooked up sometimes and had really, really great, out of this world sex. So I don't know why he's moving there." *Wrong, I know exactly why he's moving there, and I can't believe I told Shelbi about how great the sex was.*

Shelbi tried to stifle a giggle. "Yes ... I heard loud and clear. Don't worry, your secret is safe with me. Has been for almost six years. If I can go four years without telling my family I earned a culinary degree at the same time as my undergrad, I can keep this secret. And if you need to talk someone, I'm here."

"Thank you, Shelbi. I sincerely appreciate it, but there's really nothing to discuss now. We've broken it off," she said it matter-of-factly, hoping that was the end of the conversation.

"Perhaps, but Garrett has been a family friend for many years and I know him. I can't help but wonder if he's moving there to be with you. He hasn't dated anyone since you left Memphis, or at least not to my knowledge. I'll leave it be, though. I guess I've been a hopeless romantic since I married Justin."

After peach cobbler and ice cream, Shelbi said her good-byes and Zaria hung around for a while chatting with the people she used to work with before heading to her parents' home to relax and prepare for tomorrow. However, the fact that Garrett was still moving to Brunswick even after she never gave him an answer informed her he wasn't giving up yet.

CHAPTER FIVE

"Man, I still can't believe you're marrying Traci in less than two months. Hell must've frozen over," Garrett said to Sean as they tried on tuxedo jackets.

Chuckling with an amused smirk, Sean straightened his bowtie while staring at Garrett through the mirror. "It definitely did because I've been sent an angel from heaven. Honestly, I thought you'd be the first to take the plunge." Pausing, he lifted his champagne glass from the table and took a sip. "Then again, I never thought I would travel down this road, but I'll make sure to toss the garter your way so you can be next."

Sliding the snug tuxedo jacket off and grabbing one size up from the rack, Garrett shook his head with a sarcastic laugh. No need to toss him the garter. Heck, he was already married. He couldn't believe he still hadn't told Sean, but he wasn't aware of his relationship with Zaria. Sean only knew of Garrett's initial interest in her and thought that Zaria had a disdain for him. They'd agreed to keep it between them, and he respected that even though he wanted more with her. Always had. He never thought he'd fall for her in the way he did, but she was an amazing woman. He loved her ambitious and goal-oriented nature as well as her take-charge, independent personality.

Even though everyone in their circle considered her sassy with a diva attitude, Garrett witnessed a side of her that was warm and caring, almost nurturing. It was a side she kept hidden, because according to her growing up in a rough neighborhood in Memphis, she always had to keep her tough exterior on display. She refused to let anyone hoodwink her and her wall stayed up the majority of the time. Luckily, there were times when he was able to knock it down and he saw the real her.

Garrett knew she was the one for him when his mother was diagnosed with stage one breast cancer two years ago and the sweet side of Zaria came alive. He'd been stressed and miserable on the inside while trying to stay positive for his family on the outside. One evening, Zaria stopped by his home with all of his favorite dishes because he'd lost his appetite, and she'd commented that he'd lost weight. She made sure he ate and had prayed over him when he fell asleep on her lap. During his mother's chemo treatments, he would go with her and every time, he'd receive a positive, encouraging text message from Zaria. She'd even sent roses to his mother because they'd met at a few events and liked each other. Once he learned his mother's cancer was in remission, Zaria was the first person he called to thank for being supportive of him.

"You can toss the garter to one of your single cousins in Atlanta."

"Trust me, the Chase men have a little chase left in them. You know the sales lady was giving you the stare down when we walked into the tux shop. She nearly dropped the champagne glasses earlier when you smiled and said thank you. Perhaps she could be your plus one to my wedding since Traci said you RSVP'd for just you. Unless of course you were hoping to meet someone there."

Garrett's thoughts coasted back to the day the invitation arrived. He was scrolling through his cell phone contemplating who he should ask as his date to the wedding. He received a phone call from his attorney saying that the marriage license was legit, and he was indeed a married man. In that moment, he knew he had to stop playing games and make Zaria all his.

"She's cute." Garrett glanced over his shoulder and hooked eyes for a brief second with the sales lady as she helped another gentleman. She was a cutie with a pixie-cut hairstyle, long lashes, and a pleasant demeanor, but she wasn't Zaria—the only woman who had his heart. Since she'd left Memphis, he didn't look at other women the same anymore. Sure some were attractive, smart, and ambitious, but they didn't ignite a fire in him like Zaria.

"Not my type."

Buttoning up his jacket, Sean turned and faced Garrett. "That's right. You like high maintenance, feisty women like the diva."

I more than like her. "Zaria is something else. She's the epitome of what I want in a woman."

"I see, and you're um ... moving to the city where she lives." Sean tapped his finger on his chin. "Seems kind of spur-of-the-moment. Blake has asked you before to join his medical practice and

now all of sudden you're accepting his offer …
after Zaria moves there."

Garrett frowned briefly but shrugged it off.
"Totally coincidence. We've already had this
conversation. I've told you for over a year now that
I needed a change, and when Blake told me about
the position I decided to go for it."

"You do know who you're talking to, right? I'm
a psychiatrist, G. It's instilled in me to know how
people's brains and thinking process works. Plus,
you're my best friend. I've known you for over a
decade. I've seen the way you stare at her and then
try to pretend you don't care that she's not
interested. Which, by the way, I know is a load of
crap because her body language doesn't lie. And
lately … I don't know, something is off about you. I
know I've been wrapped up in preparing for my big
day and spending time with my woman, but I think
there's something you want to confide to me. I've
been told I'm a pretty good listener."

"You're paid to listen."

"I'm also a pretty good observer. So what's up,
man? Why are you really moving to Brunswick?"
he asked, folding his arms across his chest.

Chuckling, Garrett turned toward his best friend.
Nothing ever got by him for too long. But he
needed to tell someone, and of course the only
person he truly trusted besides Zaria was Sean.

"You may need something stronger than the
bubbly." Clearing the frog from his throat, Garrett
gulped down the rest of his champagne. "I'm
married." He paused, as he watched Sean's face
wrinkle in confusion. "To the diva."

"Say what now?" Sean asked a little too loud, and all eyes in the store turned on them. "When did you two get married?"

"Shh." Garrett ushered him to the back of the store behind the clearance rack and out of earshot. "You heard me correctly. She's my wife ... well, on paper anyway." He went on to explain how as Sean stared at him completely dumbfounded.

"Well, I'd figured you two had hooked up, but I didn't realize to what extent. Dang. You beat me to the altar. I'm the last one after all." A pleased smile crossed his face.

"Not so fast. She wants the marriage annulled. My attorney is drawing up the paperwork; however, I know we belong together and she does as well. It's written all over her face. She's just scared."

"Damn, first me and now you. We were players for life." Shaking his head with a sarcastic smirk, Sean placed a hand on Garrett's shoulder. "What happened to us?"

"Aren't you the head shrink with all the answers?" Garrett laughed. "I think we matured and fell in love with good women that have tested us to no end. I know Zaria has since day one, and I've enjoyed every minute of it. Trying to convince her that we're meant to be is a challenge."

"My mom says to always have faith," Sean stated with sincerity. "So, I say get your woman."

"Oh, I intend to. That's why I'm making life-changing plans."

Sean nodded his head toward the door. "No, I mean go get your woman. She just strutted in and is headed this way."

Garrett pivoted his head as his tunnel vision landed on Zaria whose, hot yet sexy expression read 'I know you just told Sean our business'. She smiled pleasantly as she approached and gave Sean a hug.

"Hello, groom-to-be. How are you?" Zaria asked with her back toward Garrett.

"I'm wonderful now that you're in town. Traci has calmed down a bit thanks to you."

"Yeah, I understand her anxiety. Most of the brides I've worked with have been stressed this close to the date, but I'm here to relieve it."

"Well, you certainly have." Sean stopped and glanced at Garrett. "So how long will you be in town?"

"I'm leaving tomorrow morning, but of course I'll be back the week of the wedding. Reagan will be here next week to meet once more with the event planner at the gardens to finalize the menu, amongst some other details."

Garrett could barely hear what they were discussing. The way Zaria's curvy hips filled out the black pencil skirt, he had to remind himself he couldn't reach out, grab her, and place a hard, deep kiss on her lips. But he wanted to—goodness he wanted to—and backed up a tad. Her sweet, sultry scent tickled his nostrils, and her hair swooped over the left shoulder was downright sexy. He had the urge to grasp her thick mane, gently pull her head back, and run his tongue over her graceful neck until she made the sexy, profound moan that always turned him on. Stifling a gulp, he took another step back. Zaria turned to him and roamed heat-filled eyes over his tux for a moment before extending a polite, but fake smile to him.

"Hello, Dr. Braxton." She said it quickly in a curt tone and faced Sean once more before Garrett could answer. "I like the tuxedos, Sean. Great choices."

"Thank you. Mine is good to go," he said, straightening the lapel." But I do have a few more I need Garrett to try on. I've decided that the best men and groomsmen will have the same tux, but the best men will wear a cravat instead of a bow tie. Not sure how I feel about this jacket, though. Do you have time to help me decide? I'm sure that's one of the reasons why Traci wanted you here. She's wants every single detail perfect, and I want my dimples happy."

"Of course. I don't have to meet the bridesmaids for another hour on the other side of the store." She nodded her head toward the frosted glass wall where the bridal store was housed.

"Great. Garrett, let's see that other one I was contemplating."

"No problem." He answered Sean but was staring at Zaria with a fox grin.

Sean's cell phone rang and he stepped away to answer it.

Garrett cracked a cocky smile. "You're beautiful as always, wifey," he whispered just loud enough for her to hear. "I'm a very lucky man." His smoldering gaze settled on her turquoise blouse, which displayed the top of her ample cleavage just the way he preferred. Noting the rise of her chest and the slight quiver of her red lips, he knew it signaled they weren't over.

"Just hurry up and try on the next tuxedo," she said through a clenched smile.

He stepped into her personal space, but this time she didn't flinch. Instead, she turned on her heat-filled stare once more. The one that hinted she was hot and bothered.

Leaning into her ear, he ran his tongue over his bottom lip that flicked briefly on her lobe. "Are you going to help me get undressed?"

Zaria stared at the man in her personal space, while at the same time holding her body still to restrain the earthquake that was ready to shudder through her when his lips brushed her skin. This man was her husband. *Her husband.* The thought still boggled her mind. He was indeed handsome in his tux, though, and she tried hard as hell to remain cool and composed especially when a part of her wanted to undress him. When she'd first laid eyes on Garrett upon entering the store, her mind drifted to the dream she had of their wedding. He'd appeared scrumptious in the dream and even more dapper and sexy in person. He'd shaven his beard off, and now a five-o'clock shadow resided. That along with the tuxedo made her blood boil, and she shoved her hands in her skirt pockets so she wouldn't reach up and kiss him senseless. However, he knew her and probably sensed that she was slowly becoming unhinged.

She had to remain composed and unbothered by his presence. She couldn't let on under any circumstances that she'd tossed and turned all last night because she knew she would see him today. Traci called yesterday evening to inform her it would just be Sean and Garrett at the fitting because Cannon and their dad were still out of the country and the two cousins in Atlanta sent their measurements to the shop earlier in the week. Before entering the tux shop, Zaria stayed in her rental car for a couple of minutes to calm down her frustrations. She knew he'd be present yet hoped that there would be others there so she could ignore Garrett, but now he was going to model more tuxedos and more than likely irk her nerves on purpose. In fact, he'd already begun.

"Boy, please." She swished her lips to the side. "No one is checking for you."

"First of all, I'm all man as you very well know. And second of all, I *will* get you back ... well, actually you're all mine now."

She had to stifle the jolt to her heart when he said the last words. He meant them and the part of her that believed in fairy tales and happily-ever-after wanted it to be true.

"Ha! You never had me, but you keep thinking that." After patting his chest, she walked away from him and a let out a quick exhale once her back was turned.

Moments later Sean reappeared, having changed from his tuxedo into a blue dress shirt and black slacks, and joined her on the comfy, white love seat in the dressing room area as they waited for Garrett.

Sean cleared his throat as he fastened his cuff links. "You know your boy is moving to the Brunswick/St. Simons area."

"Yes, I'm full aware," she answered nonchalantly while reading an email from a client on her cell phone.

"Maybe you two could be roommates," he teased. "But seriously, how do you feel about him moving to Brunswick."

Now she'd never had a problem with Sean Arrington or his family; she loved them dearly and considered them her extended family when Justin married Shelbi. However, she would hate to curse out the groom at his fitting for questioning her as if she was one his patients. And while he was a great listener and always compassionate, she didn't want to confide in him. Taking a deep breath, she turned to him and tried to hold back cutting her eyes as she so wanted to. After all, today he was her client and she didn't want to ruin anything for Traci who was a sweetheart.

Raising a curious eyebrow, a mischievous smile inched across her mouth. "How do *you* feel about that?" she asked. "After all, he is your best friend. Your running partner since medical school."

He chuckled. "Okay, I see what you did. I'll miss him, but we're both done with the ripping and running. Time to settle down with one woman ... well, at least for me, but I'm sure G will find the one for him. Maybe even on St. Simons. You and Reagan don't have any friends he could date?"

"Cut the crap, Sean. I know you know."

"I know what? That the man is smitten with you? Known that for over six years."

"Puleeze. You two looked guilty as hell when I walked in. He told you, didn't he? I know Garrett very well. It was written all over his face."

"Well ... most wives know their husbands."

She smacked her lips and pinched him playfully on his forearm. "Whatever. Not for long and *don't* tell anyone either."

"Trust me. I'm the best secret keeper in the Arrington family."

"Yet you just told her you knew." Garrett strolled out and stood in front of them. "I heard the whole conversation."

"I didn't tell her." Sean waved his hands back and forth in front of his body. "You clearly heard your wife say she knows you well."

"It doesn't matter," Zaria interjected. "This will be over with soon. Will the papers be ready before I leave?"

"No, I'll bring them when I come next week. I have some business to take care of."

"Fine. I—"

"Hi everyone," a cheery female said from behind the trio.

Zaria turned to see Caitlyn approach.

"I know I'm early, but I wanted to catch a sneak peek at the men in their tuxedos so I can give Traci the scoop, and I must say I'm glad I did. You're looking fine, Garrett."

"Aww ... thanks, Cait."

"But your cravat is crooked." Caitlyn stepped in front of Garrett and straightened it. "That's better. You know, I believe Reagan has us paired to walk down the aisle together which is perfect because I love a handsome man on my arm, and I get the best one in the wedding party." She glanced at Sean who was grinning and sipping his champagne. "No offense, Sean."

"None taken."

I know this girl is not flirting with my husband in front of me. Wait ... I mean, he's not really my husband. Okay so on paper he is, but Cait doesn't know that. We need to sign those damn papers ASAP before I believe this nonsense.

Still, heat rose in Zaria's cheeks as they continued to chat like old friends. She was never the jealous type, but it was borderline racking her nerves.

"Cait, we can head on over to the bridal side when you're ready. I'm done over here."

Caitlyn glanced over her shoulder at Zaria. "Oh sure. I'm excited to try on my dress again." Facing Garrett, she straightened the cravat once more. "Before I leave, I heard a rumor that you're moving to Georgia. Is that true?"

"Yep, I'm in the process."

"Well, we must hang out before you go. Perhaps we can have the official date we never had."

Garrett's stare flashed to Zaria's for a moment and back on Caitlyn. "Um ... that's not going to be possible. I'm seeing someone, and I know in my heart she's the one."

"Oh wow. I had no idea. Will she be at the wedding?"

Smiling wide, Garrett stepped out of Caitlyn's personal space. "She'll definitely be there. She's a very special woman to me. I can't wait for everyone to meet her."

"Congratulations. Maybe they'll be another wedding soon."

Sean snickered and patted Garrett on the back. "That would be wonderful. Wouldn't that be wonderful, Zaria? I bet G will make a loving and loyal husband."

Zaria could feel the steam rise from her head and goose bumps pricked her skin at the same time. However, she put on a sweet smile. "Yes, that would be lovely." She felt her heart betraying her for she meant those words. She agreed that he would be a loving and loyal husband. It was on her pro's list, along with protective and affectionate.

After everyone said their good-byes, Zaria spoke to the sales lady about the tux choices before heading to the other side. She was grateful when Garrett left citing the medical practice where he worked was throwing him a bon voyage party that afternoon. She didn't know how much longer she could be around him without letting her heart take the reins.

After an exhausting afternoon at the dress fitting session, Zaria headed to Rendezvous for dinner. Being with the ladies gave her brain a rest from thinking about Garrett, but now that she was alone in her car searching for a parking space in downtown Memphis, her thoughts drifted back to him. He was scrumptious in his tuxedo and his woodsy scent reminded her of being engulfed in his protective embrace.

The chime of her cell phone indicated a text message, and she almost wished it was Garrett. After finding a space a block away from her destination, she rummaged around in her purse for the phone. Chuckling sarcastically, she saw a missed message from him.

Where are you eating dinner tonight?

Headed to Rendezvous.

Meeting someone there?

Just me.

Let's go to this juke joint right over the state line in Mississippi. They have delicious BBQ.

No.

I promise I won't bring up our marriage.

And no flirting?

I can't promise that, sweetheart. You were looking mighty fine in that skirt.

Where are you?

Behind you.

Peering into the rearview mirror, she spotted his red truck behind her in the parallel parking space. He strolled over to the passenger side of her rental as she pressed the button to roll down the window.

"Are you stalking me?" she asked in a teasing manner.

"You know the medical practice is around the corner. I just left my going away party and spotted you circling the block. Let's head to my loft so you can park your car in the garage and ride with me. No point in taking two vehicles."

Once they were on their way to Mississippi, she hoped he wouldn't bring up the marriage. Luckily, Reagan and Brooklyn called for a conference call to go over details for an upcoming wedding. Being alone with him and in such close proximity shook her to the core. Not because she was scared but because she was comfortable and looking forward to spending time with him after a long day of work. She has supposed to be avoiding Garrett, but there was no place she'd rather be than with him.

A mile after passing the state line, he turned onto a dark, country road surrounded by trees. Her hand immediately went to his and squeezed it tight as she scooted closer to him.

Slowing down, he leaned over and kissed her forehead. "Relax. One of my patient's owns the place. I've been here plenty of times."

"I'm fine. It's just a little dark and wooded."

"Well, most juke joints are in the woods. We're actually on his farm. It's private. Not too many folks know about this place."

As he drove closer, she could hear the music from a live band and a man's boisterous voice on the microphone singing a familiar classic by the late B. B. King. Garrett tapped his fingers on the steering wheel to the rhythm. She relaxed and began to sway to the beat. The hickory wood aroma of a barbeque smoker filled the air and rumbled her hunger pains.

"You gonna dance with me?" he asked, parking his truck.

"Feed me first and I'll think about it." She winked and placed a kiss on his cheek as he opened his door.

"Alright, woman. Keep doing that and we won't make it inside."

Once settled at a table near the dance floor, they ordered pulled barbeque beef sandwiches, fries, and a pitcher of beer. Zaria gazed around the dimly lit, old barn house that was filled with people eating, drinking, dancing, playing pool and just having a wonderful time after a long day of work.

Their food arrived twenty minutes later, and Zaria was glad she'd decided to accompany Garrett instead of going to dinner by herself. One reason was the food was delicious but the main reason was that she truly enjoyed his company.

Taking a swig of her beer, she dabbed her mouth with a napkin. "I love this band. Wish I'd known about them when I worked at Lillian's."

"They're good. I like how they infuse blues, jazz and R&B. You know they take request. You have one?"

Shaking her head no, she bit into her sandwich.

Garrett scooted his chair back and tossed the napkin from his lap onto the table. "I have one. I'll be back, beautiful."

Moments later, he rejoined her with a pleased expression on his face.

"What did you request?" she asked curiously.

A wicked grin crossed his face. "You'll see."

After the band finished their set, the lead singer stepped to the edge of the stage and looked toward Zaria and Garrett. "My man, Garrett has a special song for the special lady in his life."

Zaria's face flushed when all eyes turned on her as Garrett stood, kissed her forehead and marched toward the stage. The singer handed Garrett the microphone, and Zaria's heartbeat raced at the anticipation of what he was about to say.

Clearing his throat, his gaze settled on her. "Z, I hope this song will make you realize just how special you are to me … how much you truly mean to me."

She placed her hand over her heart that beat a mile a minute as the band began the intro of the song "For the Love of You" by the Isley Brothers. It was the same song that was serenaded to them at the end of their Vegas wedding and whenever she heard it on the radio she'd think about her feelings for him. As Garrett began to sing the first verse, she was impressed not only by the emotion behind his words but he could carry a tune. His voice cracked a few times causing her to laugh with him. She'd never been serenaded before, and it was the most beautiful and romantic gesture a man had ever done for her. When he was done, the audience clapped and cheered while she stood and fell into his arms. Spinning her around until she was dizzy with laughter and tears, he carried her out to the dance floor as the band began to play "'Round Midnight."

"Mmm ... that was absolutely amazing. I wasn't expecting you to sing."

"I hadn't planned on it either, but when I requested it I felt the words would mean more coming from me."

"And it did. I see you aren't giving up."

A sly grin inched up his rugged jaw. "That's because you don't want me to."

"I have to say I'm enjoying this romantic side of you."

"You bring it out of me, Z."

They danced to a few more songs before calling it a night and headed back to Memphis. It was almost ten o'clock, and she'd promised her dad they'd watch ESPN. Plus, she needed to pack for her early morning flight.

"Thank you for a great time, G." She pushed the button on the key fob to unlock the car door. He opened it, and she slid into the driver's seat.

"You wanna come up?" he asked with a raised eyebrow.

"As tempting as that sounds, I made a promise to my dad. You know I'm a daddy's girl."

"You know he likes me," Garrett stated with a wide smile.

"So I heard. He said you two were partners in a spades game against Justin and Rasheed a few months ago and you two won."

"We were a great team. He's a cool old man." Clearing his throat, he stooped down to her. "So, I'll be in St. Simons soon. Spoke to my real estate and everything is good to go."

She simply nodded as he caressed her hands in his making her not want to leave.

"So … um my attorney called earlier today. The annulment papers will be ready in a few days."

"You're not making me decide at this moment, are you?" she asked.

"No. I don't want you making a life-changing decision without thoroughly thinking it over, but I do want you to think about us. That's all I ask."

"Trust me, I have and I appreciate the fact that you haven't rushed me."

"Be safe, beautiful." He kissed her softly and closed the door.

Before drifting off to sleep that night, she grabbed her cell phone and scrolled through her notes until she found the pros and cons list. She added romantic and considerate to the very long pro list and fell asleep with a peaceful smile on her face.

CHAPTER SIX

Opening the door, Zaria stepped aside to let Garrett pass, but he snatched her to him and kissed her deeply, pushing her against the door to close it.

"Hi there," he said tenderly on her lips before releasing her just as quickly as he'd grabbed her.

"Hello, yourself."

He'd arrived in St. Simons early that morning to close on his home. She hadn't seen him since their evening at the juke joint but they'd spoken on the phone or through text messages when possible. She'd been busy with an event and worked around the clock the past three days setting up and creating extravagant, over-the-top floral arrangements and place settings. While exhausted, seeing and kissing him pepped up her mood. Her busy-ness afforded her to not think about her life, and falling asleep as soon as her head hit the pillow had been a blessing. However, he still managed to enter her thoughts during any down time and looked forward to his arrival. Now that he was here, her heart was literally turning flips.

Following him into the living room, she motioned for him to sit on the couch, but she remained standing.

"Did you bring them?" she asked, referring to the annulment papers.

An amused expression washed over his features. "No, I don't want anything to eat or drink, but thanks for asking," he responded sarcastically, reaching into the folder he carried and handed her the papers.

She set them on the coffee table in front of him. "Sorry. Would you like something to eat or drink?"

"Just cold water will be fine. It's hot on the island, but I should get used to it since I do have the keys to my new home."

"Congrats." She retreated to the adjoining kitchen to grab a bottle of water from the refrigerator. "Any issues with the house considering it was bank-owned and you had to buy as-is?"

"There was a thorough inspection done. Just normal wear and tear on a ten-year-old beach house. There are some things I'm going to have remodeled, like the kitchen and bathrooms. The main issue for me is the air conditioner, but a repair guy is coming next week."

"It's the summer so you need to nip that in the bud fast," she said, handing him the water and joining him on the other side of the couch. "It's a different kind of hot here than it is in Memphis."

He raised the left side of his jaw in a cocky manner and his smoldering gaze settled on her face. Her next breath wedged in her throat.

"So … you're saying our lovemaking will be even hotter here than it is in Memphis? Glad I decided to relocate after all."

She smacked her lips and tossed a decorative pillow at him. "I was referring to the weather. The sun is no joke here."

He chuckled sarcastically. "Whew. Tell me about it. I spent the day unloading boxes from the U-Haul and sweated like a pig the entire time. The beach is right behind my house so I took a dip before I came to see you."

"So when you do you officially move here?" she asked with a slight gulp. She still couldn't believe he'd actually up-rooted his life in such a short period of time.

She noted the rise of his eyebrow as a sly smile inched up his left jaw.

"Why? You can't wait, huh?"

"Don't flatter yourself. I'm simply asking."

"I have a few more loose ends to tie up in Memphis. I don't start work for another month. However, every Saturday during the summer, Blake's staff goes deep sea fishing and I've been invited so I can get to know them and vice versa. Never done it before so I'm excited. You want to come? He said spouses are welcomed."

"I have the garden club event I've been preparing for tomorrow. Besides, I'm not your spouse." Her eyes landed on the annulment papers on the table that she noticed he hadn't signed. "Well … kind of. Finish telling me about your house."

"You wanna see it?" He stood up. "It's not far from here. It's by the Frederica Golf Club."

"Why am I not surprised? You'll be over there all the time."

"Or here …" He winked.

Swishing her mouth to the side, she stood in front of him and patted his chest. "You wish." She retreated to her bedroom to grab some flip flops and her purse "You just never give up."

"Nope, especially considering you never answered my question," he called out from the living room. "I figure it must not be a no since you didn't come out and say it. Trust me, I know you and that sassy mouth of yours. But we don't have to discuss it until you're ready."

She froze as she sifted through her purse searching for her keys. She'd hoped he wouldn't bring that up but appreciated that he respected her enough to not force her.

"You can ride with me. I'll bring you back."

"No need. I'm a big girl," she said, returning to the living room and walking toward the door with him behind her.

"It's nighttime and I want to make sure my wife gets home safely."

She tried to suppress a smile but it was no use. "I'll follow *you*. I'm not staying long. I have an early day tomorrow. So do you with your deep sea fishing outing."

"I'd rather go golfing, but I'll do that on Sunday."

Twenty minutes later they arrived at his new home and Zaria was astonished at the huge white stucco, contemporary home in front of her. It was absolutely breathtaking. She parked next to his truck in the three-car garage. Reaching to open her door, he blew the horn at the same time and she jerked her head in his direction. Exiting his vehicle, he rushed around to her driver's side door and opened it.

"When have I ever let you open the door?"

"Oh yeah." She smiled meekly and jumped down from her SUV. She'd forgotten what a chivalrous gentleman he was and made a mental note to add that to the pro side of her list. The list she couldn't believe she was still adding to. The list that didn't have any cons on it as of yet.

Unlocking the door, he glanced at her over his shoulder. "I don't have any of my furniture here just a bunch of boxes. Perhaps, you know of some furniture stores I can check out."

"Oh yes. There's some on the island and over in Brunswick," she answered as they entered the keeping room off the kitchen. "The furniture at your house in Memphis is outdated and doesn't match this house."

"Yeah, that's what I thought. You have a fine-eye for detail … maybe you can help me select some things."

"This is gorgeous." Her eyes gazed around the chef's kitchen. The cherry wood cabinets were stunning along with the black appliances. The huge island in the center could hold plenty of dishes if he ever decided to have a party. "It could use some updating, but it's still functional until you do so."

"Mmm … yeah. Whatever you think is best."

They continued walking through to the vast living area with the stoned floor-to-ceiling fireplace being the focal point. The wide-planked, walnut floors and wall of Palladian windows rounded out the elegance of the room. It was a blank slate and her creative juices were flowing.

She tapped her finger on her chin. "This house reminds me of the one we rented in Martha's Vineyard. Goodness, I loved that house. This is almost a replica. You know, I'm thinking Cape Cod style perhaps."

"Yeah, whatever you think." He shrugged nonchalantly. "I know nothing of decorating. My mom did my last house."

"How's your mom?" she asked in a concerned manner as they headed upstairs. She'd taken a liking to Mrs. Braxton having met her at Justin and Shelbi's one-year anniversary party.

"Cancer is still in remission, thank goodness. She's still feisty and full of energy. She reminds me of you sometimes."

"I like her. She was the belle of the ball at Raven's wedding. I believe your parents danced all night."

"Yeah … they're happy. Your parents seem happy, too."

"Married for thirty-five years and they're still going strong. They're best friends."

"That's how it should be," he stated, opening a door and letting her pass through.

She spotted a mattress and bed linens in the middle of the hardwood floor, which she realized ran throughout the entire home except the kitchen and laundry room.

"I'm assuming this is the master bedroom?"

"One of them. There's an in-law-suite that's almost the same size as this room downstairs. I promised my parents they'd have a room and a key so they can visit anytime. Now that they're retired I'll probably see them a lot. They love the beach."

"That's so sweet of you." She headed toward the French doors in the sitting area and opened them to a huge, covered deck that overlooked a swimming pool and the Atlantic Ocean.

"You can sit out here and drink coffee or wine," she suggested, staring out at the glistening water under the night sky. The peacefulness and tranquility of the scene before her was one of the reasons why she moved to St. Simons.

"You mean wine for you. I prefer Jack Daniels. In fact, there's a wine cellar in the basement. The previous owners left a few bottles, and I placed them in the wine fridge in the kitchen. How about we have a glass to celebrate my new home?"

"That sounds great. Can we sit on the beach?"

"Perfect, considering I don't have any chairs and its cooler outside. I'll grab a blanket and you can pick the wine."

"Do you have snacks by any chance?"

"There's some spinach dip and tortilla chips, and leftover pepperoni pizza in the fridge."

"Perfect. All of our favorites."

Twenty minutes later, they were settled on a down comforter, munching on pizza and sipping wine. She clinked his glass with hers. "Here's to your new beginning on St. Simons. It all happened so fast." She took a sip, followed by a swig.

He pulled her by the waist toward him and rested his head on hers. "I had a reason," he stated seriously. "A *very* important one."

"I know," she answered barely above a whisper. A cool breeze blew over her, but it was nothing compared to the shiver that drove through her body because of his last statement. Nestling closer to him, she wove her fingers in his when his hands rested on her stomach. He'd begun to bulldoze down her wall, and she didn't mind one bit.

He kissed the top of her hair. "Comfortable?"

"Yes. Are you? My hair keeps blowing in your face. I can pin it up."

"I prefer it down."

"I know." She stared up at the sky and noticed a few shooting stars. It had been one of her favorite pastimes since she'd moved to the island. Sometimes, she'd sit on the beach behind Reagan's home with a glass of wine and relax after a long day of weddings or other events, either with the girls or by herself. Garrett would cross her mind at times and now it seemed like a wish come true that he was actually there with her.

"Did you make a wish, babe?" he asked, moving all of her hair to the right side of her shoulder and kissing her neck tenderly.

"I did. Did you?"

"No need to. You're in my arms again." He placed another kiss to her neck, but this time it was more passionate, eliciting a fervent moan to release from her throat.

"Garrett ... can we go inside?" She turned her head to him and kissed his lips softly.

"You don't want to make love right here?"

"We've done the beach thing before when we went to Panama City. Let's christen your new home. It was one of my wishes."

He stood quickly and pulled her to her feet. "Then your wish is my command."

CHAPTER SEVEN

They rushed back to the house and onto the covered veranda that overlooked the pool. Garrett was more than elated to make her wish come true. After her not responding to his question the last time he was in St. Simons, he decided not to rush her for the fear of pushing her away. Zaria was the type of woman who rarely made a decision without thinking it through, and he appreciated that about her. He knew her well and she was letting her guard down.

"I hate to track dirt in your home," she said, stopping at the door and trying to wipe the beach sand off her legs and feet.

"There's an outdoor shower behind that wall on the other side of the outdoor kitchen. We can rinse our feet off."

A naughty grin crossed her face. "Oh really? Mmm ... let's start there." She slid her sundress seductively over her head and flung it at him, followed by her bra and panties. "Why are you still wearing clothes?" she asked, massaging her breasts in a circular fashion before swishing off in the direction of the shower.

Not wasting any more time, he tossed off his flip flops, threw his fraternity T-shirt over his head and yanked his shorts down along with his boxers. Fishing around his short's pocket he pulled out a gold packet. Rushing over to the shower, he found her underneath the rain showerhead.

"It's about time," she said, travelling her hands over her body in places he needed his hands and tongue to roam. "I had to start without you."

His eyes followed her hand down to her center as she rubbed herself and moaned his name over and over. He licked his tongue over his lips as he watched the sexy scene before him. Goodness he wanted to touch her, but he didn't want to stop her either as her fingers sunk lower and her head arched back.

"Garrett … you like that?" she asked gruffly.

"Hell yeah. You know I love to watch you pleasure yourself." He stepped closer but stayed outside of the shower.

"Mmm … it feels so damn good, G." She glided one of hands to her breast, lifted it, and sucked the nipple into her mouth, running her tongue around it as a loud hum sounded from her throat. "I can't wait for your lips and hands on me."

His penis sprung up and pointed directly at her. He didn't know how much longer he could hold out, but he wanted her to finish.

"Have you done this since we've been apart?"

"Mmm hmm. And when I climax, I always yell out your name … over and over. I shake and toss and turn all over my sheets that are drenched with sweat. I get so hot and wet thinking about you, Garrett … baby." Her hand sped up as she grinded against it and she sucked her other breast into her mouth. "Oh baby … it feels so good. I can't wait for you to take over."

"Me either. I've missed you, Zaria. "

"I've missed you … Shit, Garrett … mmm …"

He stepped closer. "You coming, baby? You gonna climax all over for me?"

"Yes, Garrett," she screamed out. "Only for you."

"That's my pussy?" he asked roughly, stepping into the shower and backing her against the wall. He placed his lips on hers but he didn't kiss her.

She gazed at him with haughty eyes as her body trembled against him. "Yes, baby. All yours. Always has been." She glided her hand from her breast down her stomach as her breathing unraveled and she screamed out. Grasping his shoulders, her body convulsed against his.

"Oh Garrett … whew. That was wonderful." She leaned her head back on the wall and closed her eyes as her breathing calmed down to normal.

"I haven't even touched you yet, but when I do trust me that orgasm will be far more explosive than the one you just had."

Chuckling, she opened her eyes and stood on her tippy toes to give him full eye contact. "Oh it better be."

Placing the packet on the soap shelf, he drew her toward him and crashed his lips on hers in a torrid kiss while the warm water cascaded down on them. Her sweet mouth on his tore shivers through him at a rapid rate as he probed his tongue deeper into her mouth. Her erotic moans turned him on more and more. He ran his hands down to her butt and squeezed it tight, pulling her closer to him as if that was even possible. She'd excited him to no end a moment ago and now it was his turn to drive her crazy.

His tongue trailed down her neck as he nibbled and kissed it. The louder she moaned the
harder he sucked.

"Stop trying to brand me," she quipped. "I don't belong to you."

Chuckling at her favorite line to say, his tongue continued its path between her breasts and he popped one hardened nipple into his mouth. "Yes you do. Every inch of you belongs to me."

"I know."

"Girl, you drove me crazy earlier."

"That was the whole idea, G."

"Well it worked, and I will drive you crazy back."

"Oh ... I know, Doc. What do you have in mind?"

He met her eyes. He knew her well; especially, when the wicked smile rose up her cheek. "Oh I see. You want to be a naughty girl tonight?"

"Yes. All night."

"Mmm ... He glanced at the towel rod. "Wait right here."

She frowned. "Hurry back."

He skedaddled up to his bedroom, to his closet and to the goody drawer, grabbed a few items that she was familiar with, and rejoined her in less than two minutes. She squinted her eyes in the dark and then they became wide with realization.

"You better have the keys."

"Relax. They're attached," he said, tossing the two sets of handcuffs on the bench and grabbing her to him once more. "Now where were we?"

Zaria turned them so his back was against the wall and kissed him hard and deep, winding her tongue around his slowly while running her hand down his skin until she reached his waiting erection. She moaned against his lips and increased the speed of their amorous kiss. Her hand continued to rub the full-length of his rod. He stifled a gulp and tried not to break their kiss, but his breathing became irregular when she slid down his body and placed her tongue on the head, circling around the tip. Resting her hands on his thighs, she engulfed all that she could in one swoop and it nearly caused him to slide down the wall.

"Oh baby," he groaned, placing his hands in her soaking wet hair and guiding her up and down. Not that she needed it. Zaria always knew how to please him. She continued the sweet torture on him; sliding her mouth as far as she could, holding for a second, and releasing all the way off of him. Her moans filled the air, and he'd always loved how she received pleasure from it as well. Her hot tongue licked up and down at a slow pace causing him to quiver with delight. Zaria knew exactly how to drive him wild and send him over the edge. Sliding her mouth on it until the tip touched her throat, she did so over and over as he met her bobbing with his thrusts until he pulled her off of him and reached down to raise her up.

"You good, old man?"

"This old man is about to remind you exactly why you've always come back for more." He turned her around and set her hands on the towel rod.

Smacking her lips, she laughed. "Don't flatter yourself. You were just lonely and available," she teased. "Probably tricked me into marrying you because no one else would."

Popping her bottom, he enjoyed it when she squirmed and looked at him over her shoulder.

"Mmm … do it again."

He obliged and proceeded to handcuff her hands to the rod. "Keep talking shit, Zaria."

"Oh, I will. I most definitely will."

Zaria breathed out as she waited with bated breath for him to continue while her body trembled with anticipation. She loved their lovemaking sessions because they were always in sync with each other, and she only enjoyed experimenting and trying new things with Garrett because she trusted him.

When she heard the rip of the packet, an ardent moan released from her throat. Moments later, his hands caressed her bottom and then travelled up her back to her neck. When his lips brushed the back of her neck, she shook and wiggled her butt against his stiff erection. "Please, G."

"Please what?" he asked in her ear.

"You know what, dammit."

"You know I hate when you curse, Z."

"Um … when am I supposed to curse?"

"Only when I'm deep inside you."

He slid into her inch by hard inch as she planted her feet firmly on the shower floor. "Uh ... oh shit, Garrett. Damn, baby ... mmm."

Grasping her hips, he pulled her slowly to him but didn't move. "I've got you."

He started out at a slow and steady pace, thrusting halfway in and out of her, sending electric bolts shooting through every cell in her body. However, with every passing moment their pace began to pick up and his thrusts delved deeper causing her to scream out curse words and his name in pleasure. She met each one, slapping her butt hard against him as the steam from the shower surrounded them in a haze.

Holding tight to the towel rod, she hated that she couldn't reach back and touch him, but it only made her desire for him grow stronger. He grasped her wet hair and pulled her head back to his. His tongue swept to hers and intertwined in a dirty dance that was in the same rhythm as their lovemaking. His thrusts became wilder and out of sync and she knew he was close to releasing with her as he pounded harder and pulsed inside of her. He shuddered wildly and let out a long howling sound before crashing his head on her shoulder. Wrapping his arms around her waist, he held her close as a few aftershock tremors shook through him.

Thirty minutes later, she found herself resting comfortably in his bed and cuddled in his embrace. She'd been so weak from their tryst that he'd carried her upstairs as she dozed off in his arms.

"I hope your neighbors didn't hear us ...well, mainly me. I was loud. Quite loud. I'd hate for the

Homeowner's Association to fine you with a loud noise ordinance."

"Yes, you were loud, woman. Luckily, the two houses on either side of me are vacation rentals. No one's in either at the moment otherwise I wouldn't have brought the cuffs."

"I'm sure someone will be there soon. The island is packed with tourists during the summer."

"Yeah, I heard." He kissed her forehead. "You're so beautiful, Z. I missed holding you like this since you've been gone."

"Mmm … me too." She turned to face him. "I missed you, too."

Pulling her under him, he kissed her forehead, nose, and lips with sweet, tender kisses that deepened with every passing second but still at a slow pace. She wrapped her legs around his waist as she held onto his shoulders while he roamed his hands over her face and back. Her pleasure moans filled the air but this time they weren't loud as before. They were barely above a whisper, but he was being so gentle and loving. It reminded her of their last time before she moved from Memphis and the emotional side returned, but she refused to shut it off. Refused to run from him. She needed this. Needed to feel his warm skin against hers. Needed to hear him whisper how beautiful she was. Needed to feel loved by the man that loved her and wanted to be married to her.

Lifting his lips from hers, she cried out a meek pout for she wasn't done with the tender kisses. He didn't say anything just stared at her with a half-smile, caressed her cheek with his finger, and kissed her forehead again. She loved his forehead kisses; they were endearing and special to her.

"What?" she asked.

"Nothing, my lady. I just wanted to stare at you for a moment. I can't believe you're here."

"Well, I can't believe you're here on St. Simons … in your house."

"Mmm hmm. I couldn't stand being away from you longer."

"Make love to me, Garrett."

He reached under his pillow and pulled out a condom, secured himself, and then pulled her legs back around her waist. This time he entered her slowly, focusing his eyes on hers. She placed her hands on either side of his face and he latched his fingers into hers. Her lips reached up to his for more of his tender kisses as their pace increased a bit but it wasn't rushed. Removing one of her hands, he kissed it and placed it over his heart.

"You feel that, baby? It's beating for you."

"I know," she whispered. "I think I've always known."

His pace and thrusts sped up, and she met them with her hips as her emotions washed over. He continued whispering how much he loved and missed her and the uncontrollable orgasm slammed through her. Clenching her legs around him tighter, she clutched his shoulders as the rush of the climax soared through her. He trembled hard against her and held her tightly around the waist.

"Mmm … I love you, Garrett. I love you so much."

He breathed out a long sigh of relief and stared at her with so much adoration that tears welled in her eyes and trickled down her face. He kissed them and smiled at her with sincerity.

"I think I just died and went to heaven, Zaria. I love you, too."

He rolled off of her but still held her close in his arms. "Can we take it one day at a time?"

Smiling, she kissed his chest and his cheek. "Yes, I'd like that very much."

CHAPTER EIGHT

Zaria eye-balled the annulment papers on the table as she sipped her coffee. Her thoughts lingered on the night before last being wrapped in Garrett's warm, protective embrace as they'd made love in his bed ... well, the mattress on the floor. She didn't care where they'd made love just as long as he was nestled in her. Blurting out that she'd loved him in the middle of her orgasm, however, shocked the hell out of her but she didn't regret it. She was glad he finally knew what she'd tried to suppress for six years. Now was the perfect time to tell him for her heart had exploded with passion and love. There was no turning back. She was ready for what he wanted, but any time before now would've ended badly. Zaria never made rash decisions, especially concerning those that would change her life drastically.

She'd spoken to him briefly after his deep sea fishing outing yesterday, but they didn't speak long because she was busy with the garden club fundraiser until midnight and had crashed when she'd returned home. Sliding her cell phone from the table, she sent him a text message because she assumed he was playing golf like he did on most Sundays.

Call me when you're done golfing. I would like to come over and chat.

You can come now. I'm home.

Okay. See you in a few.

Moments later she rung his doorbell and waited for a few minutes, surprised that he hadn't answered. A few seconds later he opened the door wearing a jogging suit, which she found peculiar considering it was eighty degrees outside, until she noticed he held a coffee mug in one hand and a tissue in the other hand. His nose and eyes were red, and he turned his head away from her and sneezed loudly into his tissue.

"You caught a cold?" she asked, walking into the foyer and rubbing his back.

He nodded and sniffed at the same. "I'm fine really. Just a little congested. I think the outing on the boat all day yesterday, not to mention our lovemaking in the shower, may have contributed to my cold. I'm glad you stopped by, though."

"Why didn't you tell me you were sick? I would've brought you something."

"I just took some cold medicine earlier. It should kick in soon."

She glanced down at his feet and realized he wasn't wearing any shoes or socks. That was probably why he was sick. *Men just do not know how to take care of themselves*, she thought.

"You're barefoot and already sick. You should at least have on some socks."

He sneezed again. "You're right. I'll go back upstairs and find some. I started unpacking more of my clothes last night, but the cold took over." He turned toward the staircase but stumbled backwards as if he'd had too much Jack Daniels to drink. "I think the medicine is kicking in … feeling a little woozy. It was the nighttime kind. I couldn't find the non drowsy."

Zaria caught him before he hit the floor and sat him at the bottom of the staircase. She felt his head and the back of his neck. He was burning up.

"You have a fever, Doc. Do you still keep your emergency bag in the trunk of your car?"

"Yeah …"

"I'll be back."

Moments later, she retrieved the bag from his car and searched around until she found his digital thermometer. Taking his temperature, she discovered it was right at 99 degrees.

"It's 99. Does that constitute a hospital visit?"

"No, babe. Look around in the bag. There should be some children's Tylenol for fevers. Give me that, and then help me back upstairs. I'll be fine."

She found it and poured the recommended dosage into the cup. Holding the cup up to his mouth, she continued talking while he gulped it one swallow. "The air conditioner is barely working. You can't stay in this hot house and sleep on a mattress. You need to be comfortable. You're coming with me. I'll go upstairs and pack you a few things."

"Whatever you say. I'll just lay here for a minute." He slid down to the floor and laid in a ball.

"Give me a minute." Jetting up the staircase, she headed to the master suite that was hotter than the rest of the house. Spotting a small, empty, rolling suitcase in the bathroom, she opened the drawers in the center island of his closet and found underwear, shorts, pajamas, and socks. She threw the items into the suitcase along with his toiletries on the vanity and ran back downstairs to find him sitting up against the wall. Kneeling next to him, she placed the socks and tennis shoes on his feet.

"Is there anything you need me to grab before we head to the car?"

"My keys and cell phone are in the kitchen."

After retrieving those items along with the phone charger, she helped him walk to the door and he leaned on her as they made it down the sidewalk to the driveway.

"Thank you. You're a ... good wife." His words were slurred as he settled into the passenger seat. She reached around and buckled his seatbelt. By the time she locked up his house and placed his suitcase in the trunk, he was snoring.

For the next two days Zaria watched over Garrett, making sure he had plenty of homemade chicken noodle soup, cool water, and orange juice to drink. He slept most of the time which she was relieved about. While she had her speech prepared she welcomed the distraction of his cold. Instead, she spent most of her time sketching ideas for her portfolio, loading pictures from previous events on the gallery section of Precious Moments website, and reading over resumes for possible event planners that Reagan wanted to interview. At around 9:00 on the second night she checked his temperature and his fever had finally lowered back down to normal. He didn't have much of an appetite, but she managed to get him to eat a little grilled salmon, his favorite Georgia shrimp, and a salad. She hated to see a man who was always so strong so weak and not able to take care of himself. After she cleaned the kitchen she realized it was time for his medicine.

"Garrett, I need you to sit up and take your medicine," Zaria said, helping him prop the pillows up. "This won't make you drowsy."

"Whatever you say, doctor," he replied, sitting up and taking the pills from her. After he swallowed them he said, "You look so tired. Have you had any rest these past two days? Every time I wake up you are sitting in that chaise lounge on your laptop. What are you doing anyway? Writing a book? All I keep hearing is the fast sound of your typing and sighs that sound like you are frustrated about something."

Exhaling, she hated to admit she was frustrated over him. "Just work."

"Have you had any sleep?" he asked again in a concerned manner. "You've taken such good care of me, doc, but you need to rest as well."

"I am fine, Garrett … I just wanted to make sure you are. You were so sick. I just wanted to make sure … you were okay," Zaria sobbed, turning away from him. She felt tears steaming her eyes. Instead, she dried them quickly and made up an excuse to check on something in the kitchen. When she returned Garrett was standing up peering around the room.

"What are you searching for?" she asked, glad to see him standing up and appearing stronger.

"The remote."

"Oh it's up here on the bookshelf." Zaria reached up to retrieve it. Turning, on the television, she handed him the remote.

He settled back on the bed and changed the channels until he landed on ESPN. "You know I could really use a bath or shower, or heck maybe even both," he teased, sniffing his underarms. "My sense of smell is starting to come back, and I don't smell so hot."

"Well, you have been doing a lot of sweating and your cold is practically gone. I guess a bath won't hurt you. That way you can sit down and relax. But not a long one. I'll let you know when it's ready," she said, disappearing into her bathroom. After cleaning the tub quickly, she filled it with warm water, Epsom salt, and bubble bath. Zaria lit a few candles and turned off the light so he could relax. She heard him step into the bathroom and she smiled slyly.

"You know, I'm glad you realized how bad you truly smell. I've wanted to tell you, but I didn't want to hurt your male ego," she teased as she turned off the water.

"Whatever, woman."

She turned around and saw him standing in the doorway naked. She gasped, for she wasn't expecting to see his fine chiseled body, and roamed her eyes over him with a wicked grin. She rather surprised that he actually had a slight erection even though he was sick, and she took at as a compliment.

"Later on, my dear. Later on." He grinned, easing into the tub with her help. Garrett closed his eyes and sighed, resting his head back on the blowup pillow that was suction-cupped to the tub. "I should feel better enough to go home in the morning."

"But the air conditioner still isn't working. You'll be so uncomfortable. Just stay here until it's fixed."

Opening one of his eyes, he looked at her with an amused smile. "The repair guy is coming tomorrow and I have to be there. So ... you're concerned about me, huh? What about Brooklyn?"

She wrinkled her nose. "What about her?"

"She lives a few cottages down from you. Wouldn't she be shocked to see me here if she stopped by? And aren't you supposed to be at work?"

"I'm not concerned about what Brooklyn thinks, and I took off work to take care of you. I worked from home. No big deal. My priority was you."

A satisfied grin crossed his face as he closed his eyes once more and slid deeper under the bubbles. "This feels nice. Thank you so much for everything you've done for me. You have a great bedside manner, Dr. Brax ... I mean, Dr. Richardson." He winked, grabbing the washcloth from the side of the bathtub. He scrubbed his arms and reached around to his back to wash it, but he was still somewhat weak.

"No problem. I hated to see you sick." Zaria took the washcloth and started to bathe his back for him. He hung his head down and continued to let her scrub his skin in a circular motion. She leaned over to reach his right side and lost her balanced. He tried to help her maintain it, but instead she fell into the bathtub, causing a big splash that put out a few of the candles. She screamed loudly.

"I'm soaking wet! My clothes are wet," Zaria yelled out, sitting in the tub with her legs hanging over the sides. When she realized her hair was also wet from the big splash she became even more upset. Garrett laughed loudly.

"This is not funny, Garrett! I just got my hair done and now it's ruined!" And then she started laughing with him because she didn't care about her wet hair or wet sundress. She was right where she wanted … no, where she needed to be.

"I'm sorry. Let me help you," Garrett said, pulling her completely into the tub and to him so that she was sitting on top of him and his arms were tightly and completely around her. She tried to move but every time she did she felt his erection underneath her. His mouth was barely an inch from hers. He was no longer laughing.

"What would you do if I kissed you right now?" he asked seductively with his lips inches from hers. "I'd hate to give you my cold."

"Kiss you back, of course," she replied as they kissed each other slowly. "I've been popping Vitamin C. I'm good."

He helped her out of her wet dress and then pulled her back on top of him. Zaria could feel his erection in between in her legs. If she moved one more inch he would be inside of her, and she didn't want that to happen without protection.

Seeing the look on her face he said, "Let's take this to the bedroom."

An hour later, their limbs were intertwined together as they lay sated on the bed staring at each other.

"I never asked you about your fishing trip. How was it?" she asked, sitting up briefly to pull the comforter over their naked bodies. Now that he was feeling better she didn't want him to catch a cold all over again.

"Well aside from the smelly fish, I had fun. I caught some grouper and a trout. The deep sea fishing company cleans the fish for you and they're in the freezer. Once I get my air conditioner squared away and some furniture, I'll have to have you over for a fish fry to thank you for taking care of me."

"That sounds like fun." She kissed his chest and settled her head on it.

"I just realized I never had a chance to ask you why you were coming over to chat the other day."

Sitting up and staring down at him, she realized she'd forgotten all about that. She was too busy making sure he was comfortable. "It's about the annulment papers."

He groaned and released a long sigh. "Oh yeah. Those," he said sarcastically. "I take it you signed them." He sat all the way up on the pillows and breathed inward.

"I did, but ... before you sigh and groan again, hear me out." A chill rushed over her as she straddled him. "I meant what I said the other night. I love you. I've been in love with you for a very, very long time. I've just suppressed my feelings because I knew in my heart I wasn't ready to settle down. I wanted to make sure that I would be perfect for you, and that I would be the best woman you'd ever have." Pausing, she smiled and a tear cascaded down her cheek. "I love you, Garrett."

He reached up and caressed her face. "I love you, too, Zaria."

"Then you'll understand what I'm about to suggest."

Frowning, he squeezed her hand. "Okay. What?"

"I want to have the marriage annulled so we can do it the right way. We had a spur-of-the-moment trip to Vegas that resulted in what we thought was a fake wedding just for the hell of it. It was a joke. We've been married for a year, we weren't aware and we weren't together. And marriage shouldn't be entered into as a silly joke. I want to be with *you* every single day that we're married. I want to come home to you, take care of you and be with my husband. Seeing you sick and helpless these last few days made me realize even more that I don't ever want to be without you, Garrett. I have to admit, when I met you I was in my I'm-an-independent-woman stage. I just wanted to work, pursue my dreams, and take care of me. And then you walked into my life and changed it in one second. I'll never forget how you strolled casually up to me wearing the most gracious and honest smile I'd ever seen. I wanted you that moment and that scared me. I had to raise my guard quick, and I started rambling about the menu, decorations, and my vision of your event just to avoid unraveling right there at your feet. And even though you wanted an actual relationship eventually, I also knew I wasn't ready for that, at least not with you. I knew you were the one, but I wasn't perfect for you then. I was self-centered and at times shallow. I wasn't ready to be someone's wife. I wasn't ready to be your wife. I knew being with you would lead to marriage and I wasn't ready. For the record, I did make a pros and cons list. There's only pros. I can't think of one reason why I wouldn't want to spend my life with you."

Garrett squeezed her hand tighter and kissed it gently. "That is the most endearing and honest thing you've ever said to me, baby."

"And I mean it. I want to be with you for infinity."

"Wow, I guess we have a lot explaining to do to our family and friends."

She nodded in agreement. "Yeah, because besides Sean ... oh, and Shelbi, no one knows about us."

"Shelbi?" he asked with a forehead scrunch. "She knows?"

"She kind of heard us having sex one time in my office."

"Oh mmm ... well, add my mother. She swears something is going on between us and hasn't liked any of the women I've brought home. She was elated when I told her I was moving here. She adores you."

"Can't say that I blame her." She giggled when he popped her butt. "Besides, according to you, I'm perfect."

"And you are. So let me get this straight. You want to annul our current marriage and get married again?"

"Yes, with our family and friends considering they've always joked we should be together. I guess they saw the love that was between us the entire time. They have to be there."

"Like a surprise wedding?"

She smiled wide followed by a loud laugh and kiss to his forehead. "Wow, that thought hadn't crossed my mind. That would be so cool. Let's do it. I can arrange it soon because I don't want to spend too long not being Mrs. Garrett Braxton once the annulment goes through. We can have it in Memphis citing my thirtieth birthday party, but after Sean's wedding. We don't want to take anything away from him and Traci. We should probably tell our parents, though."

"I agree, babe. I'll have a chat with your father soon."

She nodded. "Great idea. Oh and we'll have it at the Cultural Arts Center where we first met …"

He pulled her all the way down to him and caressed her face. "And fell in love."

Her eyes welled up with tears. "Yes, my love. Where we fell in love. I love you, old man."

"And I love you, my little diva."

EPILOGUE

"I knew it. I knew it!" Reagan shouted, giving her cousin a tight hug. "You've been overly secretive in planning your birthday party and now we know why."

"I can't stop crying!" Brooklyn screamed out. "Do you how long we've wanted you to wake up and realize that Garrett was in love with you? I'll answer it for you. Ever since you two met. That's how long!"

Zaria and Garrett were overwhelmed with family and friends rushing toward them clapping and crying as they stood in the center of their surprised loved ones barely one minute after the minister announced they were officially married.

Laughing, she hugged Reagan and Brooklyn who'd almost dropped her camera as Zaria glided out of the Cultural Arts Center when Shelbi announced the birthday girl was making her entrance. Everyone screamed when Zaria emerged on her father's arm in an alluring straight, white-laced dress and down the aisle to the lily-covered gazebo for the outdoor fall wedding. Garrett and the minister strolling over to the gazebo caused even more screaming and cheers especially when the harpist began to play "The Wedding March."

It had been the perfect moment for Zaria to see Garrett waiting for her with so much love and admiration on his face. Tears had burned her eyes as she'd walked toward the man she loved just like in the dream she had of marrying him. She'd been elated for everyone to know just how much they meant to each other and was glad their loved ones were present to share in their precious moment. It had been a long five months trying to keep their secret, but it was worth it in the end to see so many smiling faces. There wasn't a dry eye from anyone as the happy couple recited their vows followed by a deep, tender kiss that had the audience clapping and cheering.

During their first dance as husband and wife, Zaria was astonished that Garrett had surprised her with the band from the juke joint and even more elated that the song for their dance was "For the Love of You."

She smiled at Garrett as he kissed her hand. "Finally a moment alone," he said, kissing her forehead. "Well ... sort of."

They'd been engulfed with congratulations and questions for the past hour that finally Reagan took over the festivities and placed the occasion back on track.

Zaria gazed around the reception hall. "I know. I think everyone is still in shock."

"Yeah. I'm glad we decided to do it this way and be surrounded by our loved ones. They've rooted so long for us to be together."

After the dance and cake cutting, it was time for the bouquet toss. Zaria stood on the stage and looked out at the single ladies below her. One in particular she didn't see in the mix and perused again. She spotted who she'd searched for standing away from everyone else by herself. Turning her back to the crowd, Zaria inhaled, winked at Garrett, and tossed the bouquet as hard and high as possible so it would land where she really wanted it to. Pivoting back around, she was elated that it landed at Reagan's feet. Reagan pursed a smile at Zaria and bent to pick up the flowers, shaking her head the entire time.

Garrett leaned over to Zaria. "You did that on purpose, didn't you?"

"Yep. She's always carrying on about how she wants a family yet hasn't made the time to go on a date. Perhaps now this will light a fire under her."

Garrett yanked Zaria to him, dipped her and imprisoned her lips with his. "You are a mess, woman. I'm going to enjoy the rest of my life with you."

The End

ABOUT CANDACE SHAW

Candace Shaw writes romance novels because she believes that happily-ever-after isn't found only in fairy tales. When she's not writing or researching information for a book, you can find Candace in her gardens, shopping, reading or learning how to cook a new dish.

Candace lives in Atlanta, Georgia with her loving husband and their loyal dog, Ali. She is currently working on her next fun, flirty and sexy romance.

You can contact Candace on her
Website
www.candaceshaw.net

Facebook
www.facebook.com/AuthorCandaceShaw

Twitter
www.twitter.com/Candace_Shaw

BOOKS BY CANDACE SHAW

Arrington Family Series

Cooking up Love
The Game of Seduction
Only One for Me
Prescription for Desire
My Kind of Girl

Chasing Love Series
(Harlequin Kimani Romance)

Her Perfect Candidate
Journey to Seduction
The Sweetest Kiss
His Loving Caress (June 2016)
A Chase for Christmas (December 2016)

Precious Moments Series

For the Love of You
When I Fell for You (Fall 2016)

Free Reads

Simply Amazing (Arrington Family Series)
Only You for Christmas (Chasing
Love/Harlequin's website only)

Enjoy Chapter 1 from the fifth book in the Arrington Family Series,

My Kind of Girl

BLURB

Dr. Sean Arrington loves his family, patients, and the ladies. With no interest in settling down with one woman, he dates women—who like him—just want to have fun with no commitment and no strings attached—unless they like being tied up. Literally. However, when he lands his eyes on the cute-dimpled, quirky botanist Traci Reed, something tugs at his heart and he figures rules can be broken.

Traci has been infatuated with the rivetingly handsome bad boy since his mother showed her Sean's picture a few years ago. When he asks her to design the gardens in his backyard, Traci can't refuse. After they share a heated first kiss, she can't believe Sean actually has feelings for her. She's drawn to his smooth charisma and intellect; however, she's cautious for she knows he prefers his bachelor lifestyle. Can Sean prove to Traci she's his kind of girl after all?

MY KIND OF GIRL

Dr. Sean Arrington groaned as his cell phone on the nightstand blared through the bedroom. Turning over in its direction, he opened his eyes slightly and smiled at the pretty young thang next to him who has cuddled under his arm. He couldn't remember her name offhand, but he did remember the wild time they'd had the night before. Something like Amy or Amber. Maybe it was Amanda. He decided to use a universal word of endearment.

"Babe?" he asked in a groggy tone, wiping the sleep from his eyes as the phone ceased to ring.

"Yes?" two female voices answered cheerfully.

The other voice reminded him that they weren't alone, and a wicked grin crossed his face. He looked to his other side and discovered Amy or Amber's friend laid with her double D's pressed into his bare back as her big, shiny doe eyes rested on him. She was another PYT—he also couldn't remember her name at the moment—whose long, sexy legs were wrapped over his naked right thigh. The three of them had an erotic time last night, mostly the ladies as he sat back and watched. He'd met them at an after party for a local rapper's concert that he'd counseled. Going home with two models hadn't been on the agenda for the evening, but they'd flirted with him and each other all night.

"Can one of you beautiful ladies hand me my phone?"

The one closest to it slid the phone off of the nightstand and placed it in his palm.

He glanced at the name of the missed call. Mother. It was seven o'clock on a Saturday morning. She rarely called him that early on the weekend, for she knew he slept in to nine o'clock on the mornings he was able to, and a concernment formed in his head.

Sean pushed the comforter back—as bras and panties fell to the floor—and crawled up the middle of the bed. "Ladies, I need to take this in the other room."

Plopping on the leather couch in the girls' living area, he called his mother back. Sean hoped everything was okay as his heartbeat raced, and he ran his hand over his black wavy hair.

"Hello, my dear," she said in a voice that was way too chipper this early in the morning, which eased his mind of something being wrong. It also informed him she'd had her morning coffee. "I just need a favor from my other favorite son."

"You only have two sons."

"And you're both my favorites," Dr. Darla Chase-Arrington explained in a pleasant tone. "Now, you know your dad is in Nashville at Meharry this weekend for a medical conference. He drove his car and my Lexus won't start."

Relief washed over him. "Oh … I can call someone to pick it up for you."

"No need. I did that, but the only other car is your dad's Corvette, and you know I can't drive a stick shift. My orchid class starts at nine at the Botanical Gardens."

"I can take you," he said matter-of-factly. His mother and three sisters, as well as his sister-in-law, were the only women in his life that came first.

"Thank you. I'd hate to miss it."

Stepping over a lace black bra and a purple, slinky dress, he headed toward the kitchen as the rumblings in his stomach reminded him it was time to eat. "Mother, you have five children who all love and adore you. You aren't missing that class. We know you love your gardening. I'll see you around quarter after eight."

"Perfect. We'll see you then."

He opened the refrigerator and wrinkled his brow when he saw green juice in a container, a few pieces of fruit, and a box of organic cereal. He preferred eating healthy as well, but he was in the mood for bacon and eggs.

"Who is we?" *Oh great. Some of her garden club friends.* The last time he drove them all somewhere his car smelled like menthol ointment and Chanel Number Five for almost a week.

"Me and four orchids. It's the beginning of spring, so it is time to repot them. Don't worry, I have newspaper."

"They can ride, too," he said, heading back to the bedroom to grab his clothes and skedaddle. He needed to go home first to shower and change vehicles. "See you in a few."

After saying his good-bye, he slid on his boxers and jeans, which he'd found in the hallway, and jetted back to the bedroom.

The taller one with a long, jet black weave walked toward him and handed him his shirt.

"Everything okay?" she asked.

"Oh yeah. Just gotta go."

"We were hoping to cook you breakfast and maybe take a shower together," she purred, running her hand down his smooth, dark-chocolate muscled stomach. "Relive last night."

Sean flashed a smile as she buttoned up his shirt. "As tempting as that sounds, gotta run an errand with my mother, but maybe I'll see you ladies later tonight at your fashion show."

"We hope so," they sang in unison.

Sean swiped his keys from the nightstand and headed toward the door with both naked women on his heel. Quickly bidding them good-bye, he strolled to his black Porsche 911.

A few minutes after eight, Sean pulled into the circular driveway of his parents' estate in Germantown, a suburb outside of Memphis. His mother's orchids and old newspapers sat on the top step of the wraparound porch and the front door was wide open. She emerged wearing a pleasant smile that matched his and his baby sister, Bria's. Sean stepped out of his Porsche Cayenne SUV and opened the back door for the plants.

"I'll grab them," he said, running up the steps when his mother bent down to pick up the newspaper. "You just lock up and get settled."

Darla patted his face. "You're always such a chivalrous young man. You're going to be a wonderful husband someday. Just like your father."

Sean chuckled for the thought of that was just a mere fantasy.

"Yeah, maybe one day." He shrugged, grabbing the newspapers to spread out on the floor of the backseat. Unlike all of his siblings who were married and starting families, he'd rather enjoy his bachelor lifestyle. The women he dated weren't the settling down type either, which was perfect for him. Instead, he placed his focus on family, his patients, and community projects that included his concern for military veterans. Being a psychiatrist with his family's medical practice, Arrington Family Specialists, he was able to provide assistance to veterans who were suffering from Post Traumatic Stress.

At age thirty-six, Sean still hadn't found the one for him. At one point in his late twenties, he thought he had and gave up his playboy ways for her. However, when she continued pressuring him into marriage sooner than he wanted, it only pushed him away. Afterwards, he stayed clear of women who were eager to walk down the aisle. Instead, Sean preferred women who–like him—just wanted to have fun and hang out. Majority of them were in the modeling or entertainment industry, therefore they were out of town often and weren't looking for a real relationship. If she was available fine. If not, that was fine, too. He didn't want to become attached, and if he had the slightest inkling that they wanted anything more, he moved on to someone else.

"What time do I need to pick you up?" Sean asked, steering his SUV into the parking lot of the building that housed the workshop classrooms at the Memphis Botanical Gardens.

"Well, the class is only an hour and a half. Why don't you stay?"

He got out and dashed around to open his mother's door. "Nah … I'll help you carry the orchids in. I'll just go hang out at the Starbucks up the road."

Once he had the plants settled on the work table, his eyes perused the room. Most of the women were in their early fifties to late sixties. However, there was one young lady standing in the front chatting with Mrs. Carson, a friend of his mother's. He let his eyes inspect the younger woman. She was short, probably around five foot two. Her shape and stature reminded him of Chilli from the singing group TLC, and he'd always found her sexy. However, he preferred tall women with long legs for days to wrap around his waist or shoulders. At six foot three, he favored women closer to his height … but there were exceptions to every rule. The way her khaki Bermuda shorts hugged her hips and cute, rounded butt, would definitely make him change his mind. Her golden-brown, smooth body could mesh ideally next to his hard, chocolate one, and he had to shake his mind free of that as his manhood stirred at the thought.

Instead, Sean let his eyes continue to wander over her. The turquoise botanical garden shirt did nothing to hide the bountiful breasts underneath, and they jiggled when she laughed. An infectious one that was sincere and hearty. One he wouldn't mind hearing again, except the next time he wanted to give her the reason to. He loved a woman that didn't mind laughing out loud. It was the perfect way to relieve stress, and he always encouraged his patients to laugh more. Her hair was pulled back into a bouncy, curly ponytail. He had the urge to reach over, drag off the scrunchie, and glide his fingers through her dark brown tresses.

Remembering where he was, he slid into the seat next to his mother and leaned over to her ear so no one could hear him. "Who's the girl with the cute …" Sean stumbled on his words, stopping abruptly. He definitely couldn't say *butt* in front of his mother. Suddenly, the vision of loveliness rotated in his direction. He cleared his throat. She was adorable. "Cute dimples?"

"That's Traci Reed. She's the instructor for the class and a botanist here at the gardens."

"Oh … that's Dr. Reed? When you talk about her I always picture an older lady with a grey-streaked bun and glasses peering down over her nose." Not an endearing, young woman that had piqued his interest to the point of staying in the class after all. Perhaps repotting orchids could be fun. Leaning back in the seat, he placed his shades and cell phone on the table.

Darla smiled. "Staying?" she asked, waving to Traci who was on her way over.

"Sure. I mean … it's only an hour and a half. No point in leaving and possibly getting stuck in traffic or something. Then you'd be stranded here by yourself waiting for me."

"Of course, son," Darla replied, standing as Traci approached and gave her a warm hug. "Hello, dear."

Sean inhaled a pleasant, light rose scent when Traci turned into his direction, running her fingers along one of the flower pots as if she was trying not to make eye contact with him.

Was she checking me out on the sly?

"Traci, this is my son, Sean. He's going to join us today," Darla introduced, before walking toward Mrs. Carson in the front of the room.

Traci placed her cocoa eyes on his face as her dimples emerged. "Welcome, Sean. So glad you're going to participate. Are you into gardening like your mother?"

"Nope, I'm not much of a gardener, but my mom has four orchids to repot so I figured I'd stay and help."

"Awesome," Traci said, flashing a sincere smile that lit up the room and warmed his heart. "Let me know if you need any assistance. We're going to begin in a few minutes. Grab an apron and some gardening gloves from the bin in the back. Things may get a little dirty."

He caught a gleam in her eyes as he stood and stepped into her personal space, noting a slight change in her breathing. He lowered his voice so the ladies nearby wouldn't overhear.

"Nothing wrong with getting a little dirty."

Traci rushed into her office, closed the door, and leaned on it for support as she exhaled a long sigh of relief. She didn't know how she'd made it through the orchid repotting workshop without completely stumbling over her words. However, she remained cool and composed on the outside while she was flustered and overwhelmed on the inside. Dr. Sean Arrington—in all of his jaw-dropping, dark-chocolate gorgeousness—had sat in the back of her workshop repotting an orchid while she could barely concentrate.

Traci had known Dr. Darla Arrington for almost three years since she'd became her primary care physician before retiring last year. Upon learning Traci worked at the Botanical Gardens, Dr. Darla began taking her classes and eventually hired Traci to design the gardens at the Arrington estate. During that time, she'd met the daughters Shelbi, Raven, and Bria, with Raven becoming her gynecologist last year, but she'd never met Sean in person. She'd seen numerous pictures of him at the Arrington estate or on Dr. Darla's cell phone as she showed off pictures of her beautiful, intelligent children. All doctors, they worked at the family practice that their parents had started with the exception of the youngest, Shelbi, who was currently doing her residency at a local hospital. The parents had retired and the practice was ran by the oldest siblings; the twins, Cannon, a pediatrician, and Raven, an Ob/Gyn. Bria was an allergist who also specialized in holistic medicine.

Then there was Sean. Tall. Suave. Charismatic. His pictures certainly didn't capture his true essence. He was more appealing and dominating in person than she could've ever imagined. With skin smooth as butter and a well-defined, chiseled physique, Traci had the hardest time keeping her voice steady and her eyes away from his delectable face. A face she wanted to run her hand down, followed by her tongue to sample to see if his chocolate skin was indeed mouth-watering sweet. Of course she'd have to stand on her tippy toes or even in a chair to reach Sean's luscious lips. When he'd smiled at her after she had showed him how to carefully take the orchid from the pot, the heat from his stare nearly melted her to a puddle at his feet.

Traci couldn't believe her thoughts, but she'd always looked forward to Dr. Darla's picture show just to see Sean. His mother spoke highly of her children, husband, and grandchildren. Sean seemed to be his mother's favorite for he was somewhat of a wild card but had the same determination and ambition as his siblings. His mother had described him as the middle child that got away with everything but was always the first one she could depend on no matter what.

Glancing at the clock, Traci knew she needed to head to the lab to finish a project, but instead she slammed into her desk chair and breathed in to calm her nerves. It wasn't that big of a deal. *It's not like I'm going to ever see him again.* He only came because his mom was having car trouble. She'd visited the medical practice over ten times and had never met Sean in person, so the chance of seeing him again was rare.

A light knock at the door interrupted her train of thought which she was grateful. *Time to get back to my day and stop focusing on a man that has barely given me a second thought.* Besides, she knew his type. Playboy. Love ''em and leave ''em. She'd been there before and was so over it.

"Come in," she yelled out. She had a few minutes to spare, and more than likely it was her co-worker and best friend since college, Caitlyn Clarke, probably coming to ask who was the fine specimen she had spotted when she'd peeked into the workshop earlier. She'd done a double take and almost spilled her coffee.

Traci reached for the paperwork she needed to go over with Caitlyn.

The door swung open and the knot in Traci's throat from earlier returned when Sean breezed into her office as if it was a natural task he did every day. His confidence level was off the chart, and he seemed to be comfortable in whatever situation he was placed in. She'd noticed that earlier during the class.

"Hey, Traci."

"Hi, surprised to see you. Is everything okay?" she managed to say in a professional tone even though the butterflies in her stomach were having a break dance contest.

"Yeah. Mom decided to have lunch with Mrs. Carson. I just had a quick question."

"Oh sure. What can I do for you?"

A sexy smile inched up his chiseled face and she held back a gulp

"I know you designed the gardens at my parents' home. I recently bought a new house, but the backyard is ... um ... well, just green grass. I spend a lot of time outside relaxing on the veranda after a long day of dealing with patients, but I have nothing exquisite to look at. Think maybe you can hook it up like you did for my mother?"

Traci was still in such shock from him standing in her office that she'd barely heard what he'd asked. Nodding her head, she pretended as if she'd comprehended the words. When she replayed them, she was able to answer him.

"Well ... I honestly didn't do it all alone. I have a crew I work with depending upon what you request, and your mother helped. She's very hands on."

"Sooooo you want me to be hands on, too?" Sean stepped closer to her desk while resting a smoldering gaze on her face that she knew had to have turned scarlet for her cheeks were burning.

Traci was thankful she was seated so that he wouldn't notice her squirm, or the crossing and uncrossing of her legs. She was at a sudden loss of words. She couldn't place whether or not he was spewing sexual innuendos because he was so serious in his tone and expression. Perhaps it was just wishful thinking on her part because she'd had a crush on him since Dr. Darla had shown her his picture a few years ago.

"Not necessarily. It just depends on the client and their schedule. Your mother was semi-retired, so it was easy for her. Plus, she loves gardening. I'm convinced if she wasn't a doctor she'd be a master gardener."

He nodded his head. "Yeah, it's my mom's hobby, but for me I just want something peaceful to gaze at after a long day of work. Can you do that for me? My mom said you have a busy schedule, but I'd love for you to design and landscape my yard."

She honestly didn't have time, but for some reason she couldn't say no to him. Not only that, but she needed the extra money.

"Then I'm your girl."

Sean raised an eyebrow as his smoldering gaze reappeared, and the words she'd just stated replayed in her brain. Traci could sense a sexual innuendo running rampant in his head that would have her questioning whether or not saying yes was such a great idea. She decided to speak first before whatever was on the tip of his tongue came out and left her even more flustered than she already was.

"When would you like to begin?" she asked, taking out her iPad to look at her schedule.

An arrogant, sexy smile lined his rivetingly handsome face. "I'm ready whenever you are."

Made in the USA
Columbia, SC
13 April 2018